"All I want to know is where Seth's house is," she said quietly.

"I know where it is," I said. "Seth took me there. What does it matter to you?"

"It doesn't. I was just making conversation. Look, sweetie. I'm sorry if I hurt you and got you into trouble with Seth. You're a darling girl, and I want to make it up to you. So I'm telling you this: Go to your brother's farm. You can make things up to Seth there. Prove you're no little pest of a girl."

I was about to come back with a sassy reply when the building seemed to tremble. It shook for about three minutes. "An earthquake," Amanda Selvey said.

"No, this place is falling down!" yelled Chloe Fletcher. She was not joking.

I opened my mouth. No words came out. My whole being shook. The walls trembled, and the floor bucked. Some girls were screaming. The door to the Yankees' room blew open and a guard yelled in to us. "Come on. Get out! Now!"

JULIET'S MOON

Ann Rinaldi

GRAPHIA

HOUGHTON MIFFLIN HARCOURT
Boston New York

www.hmhbooks.com

The Library of Congress cataloged the hardcover edition as follows:
Rinaldi, Ann.
Juliet's moon/Ann Rinaldi.
p. cm.—(Great episodes)
Summary: In Missouri in 1863, twelve-year-old Juliet Bradshaw
learns to rely on herself and her brother, a captain with Quantrill's
Raiders, as she sees her family home burned, is imprisoned by Yankees,
and is then kidnapped by a blood-crazed Confederate soldier.
I. United States—History—Civil War, 1861–1865—Juvenile fiction.
[I. United States—History—Civil War, 1861–1865—Fiction. 2. Brothers and
sisters—Fiction. 3. Self-reliance—Fiction. 4. Clark, Marcellus Jerome,
1844–1865—Fiction. 5. Guerrillas—History—19th century—Fiction.
6. Orphans—Fiction. 7. Missouri—History—19th century—Fiction.] I. Title.
PZ7.R459Jul   2008
[Fic]—dc22   2007030378

HC ISBN 978-0-15-206170-8
PA ISBN 978-0-547-25874-4

Text set in Adobe Garamond

Printed in the United States of America
DOM 10 9 8 7 6 5 4 3 2 1

This is a work of fiction. All the names, characters, places, organizations,
and events portrayed in this book are products of the author's imagination
or are used fictitiously to lend a sense of realism to the story.

For my daughter-in-law, Lori,
who is always interested in my work

PROLOGUE

Summer 1863

MY SECRET hiding place in the woods saved me and Maxine the day the blue-bellied Yankees came through and fired our house and barn, ran off the cows, horses, and sheep, destroyed the fields of wheat and corn, and chased away all the negroes.

"Go, go," my pa yelled, "run."

I stood there in the barnyard with him and Maxine, feeling the rising heat of the terrible yet fascinating flames that were now eating up the blue afternoon sky above our heads.

"Where?" I asked dumbly. "Where should I go?"

"To the woods. Take Maxine with you."

"To the woods?" I repeated. I could, when the occasion warranted it, be very stupid.

"To your secret hiding place," he urged.

I didn't even think he knew about my secret hiding place. He stood there, holding his rifle. The Yankees were returning from setting the fields afire.

"I can't leave you, Pa," I said. My voice broke.

"Go," he said again. His voice was strong, like it was when he "held forth" at the table some nights on Mr. Lincoln or states' rights, and Seth and I listened because we were too scared not to.

"You won't be alone for long," he said. "Seth isn't far away. He'll see the flames and come home. Remember what the Bible says: 'And your children will meet the enemy at the gates.'"

"Oh, Pa!"

"GO!"

I took Maxine's hand and we ran.

Chapter One

L IKE I SAID, my secret hiding place saved me and
Maxine that day, just as I used to fancy it would. I'd
stocked it well with sugar cookies, slices of smoked ham,
even tins of food like Seth used in his guerrilla unit when
he fought with Quantrill and his Raiders. Maxine, our
house nigra, cook, and all-around friend to Seth and me,
had given me a stone jar of water, pillows, and blankets
to make it comfortable.

And, of course, I had my box of treasures: marbles
I'd won from Seth at our last game; a blue feather from
a peacock; one of Pa's cigars, unsmoked, that I'd stolen
from his desktop; some quills for a pen; a set of teeth

from an animal that I like to think was a baby dragon found by the creek in back of the house; and my mother's good pearl necklace that she gave me when I turned twelve. Right before she died.

Maxine was having some difficulty climbing the ladder to the tree house. I had to help her up. We spent the rest of the afternoon there. We ate the cookies and ham. We could see the house from where we were, disappearing in the smoke, belching flames from its windows.

And Pa, standing there alone one minute, alone in the barnyard, like he was cleaning his rifle, but waiting for the Yankees to return from the wheat fields. And in the next minute lying at the feet of the Yankees. Shot.

I didn't love Pa. I never had. Not like I loved Mama and Seth. Pa was gruff and had a quick, hard hand to slap and no patience with a little girl. Seth knew how to handle him; I didn't. Seth even bad-mouthed him, jokingly, calling him an old codger or some other term that Pa never seemed to mind. If I did that, I'd be put in a closet in the cellar and made to wait there until Seth talked him into pardoning me. Then Seth would come down and get me. "Don't you know any better?" he'd say as I clung to him. "You can't talk to him like that."

"You do," I'd sob.

Though they had their fights, Pa gave Seth freedom to "sow his wild oats" and would lecture him at the table the next morning. Seth yes sir'd and no sir'd him to death.

"He'd be disappointed in Seth if he didn't sow his wild oats," Maxine told me.

Once, when Seth didn't get home by four in the morning, Pa sealed up the house. Locked him right out. Seth came rapping softly at my window and I let him in. I got time in the cellar closet the next day, and Seth had to talk him out of my punishment.

I know Pa didn't like girls. I know he'd wanted another son, instead of me. And he never let me forget it. For fatherly affection I went to Seth. Pa didn't care at all.

Still, Pa shot! It was outside the realm of all family pettiness. He was still my father. Shot for what? For not giving out the whereabouts of his son's guerrilla army unit? For not telling where their cache of ammunition was stored?

I shivered. Maxine put a blanket around me. "Pa's dead," I told her.

"I know, chile."

"I'm an orphan. Will the authorities put me in an orphanage in Kansas City?"

"Ain't no orphanage in Missouri will take you."

"Am I that bad?"

"No, 'cause you ain't an orphan. You gots your brother, Seth."

"But he goes away to war."

"Seth ain't gonna let anybody take you away. Not while he lives and breathes. Now you're just a little girl. You just twelve. Seth is all of twenty-four. He old enough to care for you, even though he go to war. He gots me to see to you while he's gone."

I hugged her. "We got to bury Pa."

"We wait for Master Seth," she said.

I looked up at her. "You call him 'Master Seth' now."

"Thas' right. Thas' respect."

"Do I have to respect him, too?"

"Wouldn't hurt none if'n you did."

I giggled. "He'll still swing me around, won't he?"

She sighed. "Chile, it's a different world out there now. I wouldn't count much on anybody swingin' you 'round."

I sobered. "I wager he would if I asked. Wouldn't he?" All hope was gone from my voice.

Maxine sighed. "I wouldn't ask, honey. I jus' wouldn't ask."

We were quiet for a while. The hours passed. I decided I didn't like this world anymore. What kind of world was it if I couldn't ask Seth to swing me around? The fire was down to smoldering and the afternoon blue turned to gray and my eyes stung from the smoke. My house was gone, my room gone. I wondered how the flowered bedspread had burned, if the dolls had stopped smiling, if my dresses and shoes had taken it well. I wished I had a newspaper so I could read about Sue Mundy. They had stories about her every day and I followed her doings avidly.

She was the only woman who rode with William Clarke Quantrill, the notorious leader of Quantrill's Raiders. You couldn't pick up a newspaper but there she was, in her women's attire, sometimes in her men's attire.

She fought as a man. Seth fought with her. But he would never talk about her.

I wondered what made her do what she did. If she ever had anyone to swing her around when she was a child.

We waited for Seth to meet us at the gates.

Chapter Two

I FELL ASLEEP as the air around us thickened and the woods pulsated with things that were not to be seen. Likely in those woods were loose animals and our own negroes, hiding from the Yankees. Negroes could be stealthy. They could disappear from you in plain sight inside the house. I had personally seen them do it. Me, I could never hide from anybody. When I'd done mischief, no matter what pains I took to conceal myself, I stood out like a cut on Seth's face that he'd made shaving.

I slept right through it all, like I was dreaming it, until I heard that voice.

"Juliet? Hey, Juliet."

Seth. Waking me early to go riding with him. Or to see a newborn foal in the barn. I stirred myself, and awoke to the gray haze. I coughed, sat up. Seth was below me on his horse. He was wearing all his fighting gear, from the high-topped cavalry boots into which he'd tucked his pants, to the gray shirt Martha Anderson—his sometime sweetheart—had made for him, with the red embroidered stitching and all the pockets for ammunition.

He had four revolvers tucked into his holsters and wide leather belt and another four on his finely bred horse. He looked like a knight in one of my books. He was lean but broad of shoulder, over six feet and at ease in his own body, clean shaven, with a mouth that Martha Anderson teased "curled up even when he wasn't smiling," so that he didn't look threatening, no matter how many guns he wore.

From beneath his wide-brimmed hat he looked up at me with those sad eyes of his, which were fringed with black lashes any girl would envy.

Still, he was shy enough for girls to be smitten with him at first glance. But he was *my* brother. And he better make sure he always knew it.

"Juliet, you all right?" he asked.

"She be fine, Master Seth," Maxine told him. "I been keepin' an eye on her."

And then it all came tumbling down on me. The Yankees. Pa dead. The house and barn burned. The animals and servants run off. I started to stutter it out to Seth, but the tears came too fast and before I knew it, I was sobbing and feeling five years old again.

Sue Mundy was forgotten. Especially when Seth reached both arms up to me. "C'mon down, baby."

I went to him, let him enfold me in his strong arms. He set me in front of him on the horse, so close I could hear his heart beating and smell the woodsmoke, tobacco, and rum on him. *Traitor,* I told myself. *You like playing the little sister after all.*

"Take the mule, Maxine," he directed. "It's the only animal I've been able to find on the place."

"It's Bleu," I reminded him. Bleu was known for his stubbornness. Only Seth could control him, not even Pa.

"I'd like to see the welcome he gave the Yankees," Seth said. "Wonder how many he kicked. Surprised they didn't shoot him."

"Haven't you seen my Caboose?" I asked Seth. Had the Yankees shot him? My beloved horse?

"No, honey. Likely he's with the others in the woods. When they get hungry, they'll come back."

"To what?"

"I've alerted the negroes in the woods to bring them to my place. It's where they'll go, too."

"Can we go there now?"

"No. I'm taking you to the Andersons."

"I don't want to go to the Andersons."

"I'm afraid what you want doesn't come into it now, Juliet," he said with mild firmness.

As we neared the house, Maxine reminded him. "Master Seth, we've got to bury your father."

"It's all taken care of. Did it soon's I got here. You two were both sleeping so I didn't want to disturb you."

"Did you bury him next to Ma?" My voice quivered.

"Yes." He squeezed my shoulder. "And at the proper time we can come back and say some prayers over their graves. And leave some flowers."

"Pa didn't like flowers," I reminded him. "He said they made him sneeze."

"Well, right now the flowers are for us more than for him, Juliet," he said quietly.

"Seth, I was hoping we could go to your new house,"

I pushed. "I've never been there. But I heard about it from Pa."

"What did you hear?"

"That it's deep in a hollow and you need a map to find it and it's a lot like this one and it's probably where you take all your ladyloves."

He sighed. "I have only one ladylove and she's too much of a lady to go there with me until we're hitched proper-like."

"Martha Anderson," I said.

"And how do you know so much?" He poked me in the ribs.

"A person could be an owl in daylight and see that much," I teased. "Anyway, Pa said you strung her along too long while you ran around with your fast women."

He sighed again. "Without his help I couldn't have built that place, the mean old codger," he said.

"You're not supposed to talk that way about the dead," I scolded him.

"Why not? I talked that way about him when he was living. And he knew it, too."

I started to cry again. My shoulders shook.

"Here," he said, "you're exhausted. Your spirit is worn

down. Lean your head back and let the horse's gait rock you to sleep."

I leaned back on him. "Seth?"

"Umm?"

"Maxine says I have to respect you now, 'cause you're all I've got. Is that right?"

"You just mind what I say and we'll be all right. No need for me to pull rank on you."

"Do I have to call you Master Seth, like she's doing?"

"You do and I'll build a closet in my house and put you in it."

"So what will you do if I'm bad?"

"You planning on it?"

"Well, I can't be good *all* the time. I'll get the ague or something. I can't promise you that, Seth."

"Not asking you to promise me anything. You just be yourself. We have any trouble, we'll work it out between us. That all right with you?"

I sighed, contented, and said it was.

Chapter Three

NEXT THING I knew we were at the Andersons'
place. One of the prettiest farms in Jackson
County, after ours.

The girls, all at different stages of attractive, came out
to meet us. Martha was eighteen, Mary, sixteen, Fanny,
fifteen, and Jenny, fourteen. Their older brother, Bill,
twenty-four, also fought with Quantrill but hadn't come
home with Seth.

The girls crowded around me and Seth, their questions about the Yankees urgent and half scared, until
Martha insisted we be ushered into the house and given
some vittles and hot tea.

Their mother had died a few years ago while giving birth to a baby who had died, too. Their father was shot last year by a man named Baker, who had been courting Martha, but who, at the last minute, refused to wed her. Martha's father went to the man's house with a double-barreled shotgun the day Baker was to marry his new love, a schoolteacher. That's when Baker shot him.

The wedding went on.

Martha never got around it. Her embarrassment and shame at being put aside by Baker knew no end. And Seth, with whom she'd always been friends, was there to comfort her. I think that's when she became smitten with him.

Maxine told me all about it.

"Your brother gots his wild side," she told me, "an' he gots to find women to satisfy it, even while he love Martha."

I didn't understand it all, of course. I was only ten or eleven at the time. But the words stayed with me and I always looked for, and never found, this wild side in Seth. I'd watch him when he didn't know it, when he was cleaning his rifle, or strumming his fiddle, or brushing down his horse, or just leaning back in a hammock in the sun, and I'd wonder: How do men go about showing their wild side? If Martha knew about this wild side, she never complained.

"I know," she told me once, "that he loves me. And I'll wait for him."

In all of this, she'd made me her confidante. I was to tell her if Seth spoke as if he was getting serious about somebody. I promised her I would.

"They're a caution together," I'd once told Maxine. "They pick up each other's thoughts and finish each other's sentences. It's as if they're married twenty years already."

"You got that right, honey."

"So why don't they go and do it, then?"

"Bad times right now. Martha still has to work off some of her guilt"—she was counting reasons on her fingers—"an' that wild side o' your brother must still be lookin' at somebody."

"Who? He sees just men in his unit."

She looked at me and I at her. And then the notion came to me. And I thought, *Oh Lord God no.* I waited for Maxine to say the name, but she didn't. So I did to myself.

Sue Mundy.

My HEAD was pounding and I wished the Anderson girls wouldn't cackle so. But I sat decorously on the couch in the parlor and sipped my tea and ate my meat sandwich.

Seth had pulled me close to him because I had started crying again. And I heard his words like a rumble in his chest. "Pa dead. House and barn burned. Negroes run off."

"Well, you can stay here, of course. We have room," Martha was saying in that voice of hers that always sounded as if she were telling a story to a child, so melodious and comforting.

It was Maxine who put her hand to my forehead. "She burnin' up, Master Seth."

He took the tea and sandwich from me and lifted me into his arms. "Show me where to put her," he asked Martha. And then I passed out.

WHEN I AWOKE, I was in a pleasant room with organdy curtains and a canopied bed. In spite of the fact that it was early August, a low fire burned in the grate. I was up to my chin in sheets and a light blanket, and at the foot of the bed Seth and Martha were conversing in low tones, as if they were my mother and father.

I wished they were. I wished they were wed and I was living with them.

Seth came over to the bed. "You're awake," he pronounced.

Outside the sun was setting. He'd taken off all his

guns when we came in, allowed himself to be petted and fussed over by the Anderson girls, but now he had the revolvers on again. From downstairs came the whiff of food. He'd been fed and rested. He was ready to leave.

"You're going back," I said.

"I have to, Juliet."

Tears came to my eyes. He reached out a hand and wiped them away. "You stay here and mind Maxine. And Martha. They're both good people. Help out. Make yourself useful. I'll be coming home from time to time. You hear?"

I took his hand in both of mine and held on to it. "Don't do anything funny," he warned.

"Like what?"

"You know what I expect from you. I gotta go now." He leaned down and kissed my forehead, then took Martha by the elbow and led her out into the hall. From my bed I could see him kissing her, long and not just once. He'd end the kiss and they'd say a few words and he'd start in again, and then they commenced to walk down the stairs.

I was proud of my brother. He sure knew how to kiss. He wasn't rough with her. He was tender.

And now he was gone. I went back to sleep.

Chapter Four

I SLEPT FOR two days.

I was conscious of Martha moving about me, spooning soup into my mouth, helping me to the chamber pot, washing my face and talking to me, all the while in that storybook voice of hers, as if all of this was going to have a happy ending. I recollect her telling me that her sisters went out riding by our house and it was still smoldering. And that my horse had been wandering loose nearby, so they'd thrown a rope around him and brought him here.

He was, at this very moment, overstuffing himself with oats in the barn.

"Don't let anybody be mean to him," I said as I started to cry. I had the jimjams.

I wanted to go to the barn and see him. He must be dirty, I told Martha, but she promised me that Jenny would brush him down. That afternoon Jenny came up to my room to report on Caboose, who was doing fine. And then, she very carelessly slipped this into the conversation:

"Oh, the boys are coming home. It would be so nice if you could get up and get dressed."

"When?"

"Tonight. And you'll never guess. They're bringing Sue Mundy."

Sue Mundy! "But I have no clothes! Everything I had, except for the dress I wore here, was burned."

Jenny, at fourteen, was the closest to me in age and size. We had sometimes traded dresses, and her brother, Bill, who was Seth's age, often said how much we looked like each other. She loaned me a calico dress sprigged with pink flowers and helped me arrange my hair. I had straight hair, brown and shiny. And with a dimple in my chin and an upturned nose and big eyes, I had been told by Seth that I was pretty, at twelve. While I knew he was proud, I also knew he felt that he had to "keep tight reins on me."

"I'm in for some fun times," I once overheard him tell Martha. "She's got the men's eyes already." But he was joking. Or was he?

At twelve I didn't even get my woman's time of the month yet. But I had bosoms. Though small, they were respectable.

I was a bit shaky on my feet as I helped Maxine and Martha and the girls prepare the supper and get it on the table.

And soon they came, riding into the yard in a cloud of dust, causing dogs to bark and chickens to scatter. I saw them dismounting, taking their Sharpe's rifles from their horses, and giving those horses over, with instructions, to the stableboys. Laughing and joking they were, backslapping and cussing, as men do.

In the middle of all of it I saw Sue Mundy, with her dark hair tumbling out of her Confederate hat. She wore a full Confederate uniform. She washed up at the outside pump with the rest of them. Martha had brought out soap and towels for all.

The men poured water over their hair. They took off

their shirts; they shaved, propping mirrors up against the front fence posts. They reached for clean shirts from their saddlebags. I could not stop staring at them through the kitchen windows.

Martha gave me a small spank on my bottom. "You going to cut that bread or stand there and stare all day? Didn't you ever see your brother without his shirt?"

I had, but browned and broad as he'd been, Seth hadn't quickened me like this. He was my *Seth*, my *brother*, for heaven's sake. It was the others I was looking at. I was becoming conscious of men and I felt myself blushing.

They came in through the kitchen door. Martha made them stomp the dirt off their feet and check their rifles just inside the door, but she never made them remove their revolvers. She knew better.

Seth introduced Martha and then me. "My intended," he said, and then, "my little sister."

I knew Bill Anderson, whose sisters were now hanging all over him. But Lord knows I'd never met William Clarke Quantrill. And he was nothing like I had fancied him to be. He was blond haired and wore a slight mustache. Otherwise he was clean shaven and polite. He bowed to the ladies. He kissed Martha's hand.

I bobbed a curtsy at him and he said, loudly, "You got a fine little sister here, Seth. Any time you get tired of takin' care of her, you can send her to me."

"No chance of that," Seth answered, but I could tell he was trying to figure out if Quantrill was joking or if he was serious.

I met two young brothers called Younger and another callow youth called Jesse James. He couldn't have been more than sixteen. All of them seemed to worship Quantrill and hung on his every word.

And then I met Sue Mundy.

"Hello." She stuck out her hand and I took it, not quite believing I was shaking hands with the woman I had admired and read about for so long now. Her grip was firm. Her eyes were friendly. She had pinned her hair back neatly and she could easily pass as a young Confederate soldier.

"I've always admired you," I said, for lack of anything intelligent to say.

Somebody gave out a whoop. "Gawd Awmighty, Seth, didn't you train her up any better than that?"

Seth blushed. "C'mon, everybody, sit down. Bill's gonna say grace."

"If'n Bill Anderson says grace, I ain't gonna eat none of the vittles," said one of the Younger brothers.

"Come sit over here next to me," Seth directed.

There was an empty chair next to Sue Mundy and I wanted to sit there. But everyone else was seated and I was holding up the meal. And all were waiting for me to make my move. I had to obey Seth or he'd never live it down.

I didn't want to. Good Lord, did the first set-to between us have to be with half the Confederate army looking on?

It lasted only a second or two. But it was written across the face of eternity. My brother, who raised his expressive eyebrows in my direction, saying nothing anybody could understand but me.

I went around the table and sat next to him. Did everybody sigh, or was it my imagination? They all started talking at once.

"Quiet now," Quantrill said, "you heathens. And let Bill say grace. It's his house, his table, his food, and his sisters who cooked it. Let's have some respect."

Quantrill had spoken. They all fell silent. Bill said grace, making it personal, saying something about my pa and adding a bit about all the boys who'd fallen at Gettysburg.

The food was scrumptious—rack of lamb, four chicken potpies, a side of beef, browned potatoes, about every vegetable known to man, roast pork, and three kinds of cake for dessert.

The men stayed a week—to rest, eat, play chess and cards, dance with us girls, play their instruments of music, groom their horses, race their horses, make cartridges, clean their guns, and sometimes just lie in the sun with their shirts off.

They helped with the chores: chopping wood, hunting for fresh game, fishing in the creek, stocking the meat house, picking the tomatoes and beans and corn and anything else that needed picking.

Even Sue Mundy worked. I saw her working, side by side, with my brother in the fields. And there was something between them, my brother and Sue, some lightning when words were exchanged. I saw Seth blush more that week than ever before. I saw him go shy in front of her, and that meant he liked her. I know Martha saw it, too.

At the end of the week the whispers started to go

'round like the night vapors that the men were planning another raid. Not even we girls were told where.

In that week, Seth asked me to take a ride with him to go and see his house. I knew something was coming, but I could count the stars in the sky before I would venture to guess what.

Chapter Five

THE DAY was a quiet blue one the second week of August when we rode to Seth's house. He got right to the point.

"School soon," he said. "What'll we do this year? Damn Yankees are all over the place. I've talked to Martha. She agrees that if you girls go, they can walk right in your schoolhouse and gather you all up in one fell swoop."

"Why would they want to do that?"

"Don't know. But any time all the kin of the enemy is gathered in one place the enemy is vulnerable. Martha is keeping her sisters home. Goin' to head up their lessons there. You want to be part of that?"

"Do I have a choice?"

"No."

Martha as a teacher. There was a new thought. "Martha's my friend," I said.

"I expect you to learn nevertheless. No foolin' around. Martha can be a stern taskmaster."

"Don't you like her anymore?"

"Say what?"

I repeated my question. He frowned. "First place, it isn't any of your business. Second place, it's the dumbest question I ever heard. This is Martha we're talking about."

"I caught her crying after supper in the kitchen. She thinks you're smitten with Sue Mundy."

He stared straight ahead. "And what did you say?"

"Nothing. I didn't say anything. Because I don't know, the way you've been sweet-talking Sue all week. What's a person like me to think?"

"A person like you is to mind her own business."

Something in the way he said it made me decide that I never wanted to get on the bad side of him. Ever.

"Some say Sue is a man and some say she's a woman," I reminded him, giving the conversation a new turn. "To me she's a woman and a heroine. Like Joan of Arc."

He scowled. "I've noticed how much time you've spent with her this last week. Don't make friends there, Juliet." He was begging. "There are other girls I'd rather have you emulate."

"Who?"

"Martha."

So he still did think highly of Martha. We were at the path that led to the holler now. From the distance you could hear echoes of hammering through the thickness of the trees. He slipped off his horse and gestured that I should do so as well. I did. Then I followed him down a steep path into the valley, where there was a trickling stream at the bottom. A narrow wooden bridge straddled it. I expected to lead my horse across, but we just stood there on the bank while the horses watered.

"You can't even see it from here for the trees," I whispered to him. "All I can see is some big sprawling thing with fences and a porch and"—I stood on tiptoe—"why, it looks just like ours did, Seth!"

"Does that surprise you?"

"No, I guess not."

"I've got everything Pa had. Parlors, big windows, an office, a nursery, I've even got a room for you. Upstairs. It's just that it's made of logs."

"Really? Could we go see it now?"

"No," he said. "Leave everyone to their work. The negroes we had at home are harvesting the corn and wheat and just about everything else. I've had some of them here working all summer, with Pa's permission. Now Maxine's stepped in as overseer."

"Maxine?"

"Don't laugh. She could put on a tall hat and be Lincoln, that woman. Look, I just wanted to let you know how to get here in case you need to someday."

"Why would that be?" I pushed.

We led our horses back up the hill. "If the Yankees come and fire the Anderson place. Or just run you girls off. Or if, in any instance, you just need a place to stay. I'd want you to bring the others here. Promise me that, Juliet."

I knew what he was doing. Providing, in case something happened to him. "I promise," I said.

"And, if I fall in a fight, I'd like you to stay in this house with Martha and her sisters. It's got everything you all will need. Course, it'd be your house then." He cleared his throat. "I've made some arrangements."

"Seth, are you going to die?"

He grinned. "Course not, honey, I'm too pumpkin-headed, toad-rotten mean to die."

"I don't think you're mean, Seth."

"Then let's hope I never have to be mean to you, honey. Look, anybody with half a brain has got to make arrangements. I've a lot to think about now. My wild days are over."

"Are you going to marry Martha?"

He had the decency to blush.

"I've never kissed Sue," he said quietly. "I promise you that. But God help me, I am smitten with her. There's something about her that can bewitch a person. But I never kissed her or put a hand on her. Tell Martha that for me, will you, please? I know you two talk and tell secrets."

"Yes, Seth, I'll tell her." Proud to be confided in, I was. Proud that he trusted me, this brother of mine. And I wanted to say something to let him know how much I loved him. And all the rest of it was teasing on my part. But he knew it, I was sure. Brothers always did, didn't they? When it came right down to it, when push came to shove, they'd die for you, wouldn't they? Bill Anderson's sisters knew that about Bill, and I would know no less about Seth.

We rode back to the house in near silence. There was nothing more to be said.

Chapter Six

THE MEN left at five the next morning, just as old Caesar, the rooster, was welcoming the day, which was as yet all mist. I heard muffled talk, laughter, from downstairs. I smelled coffee and bacon. I put on my robe and slippers and crept down to see them all huddled around the dining room table, still using lamplight, which, in itself, cast long shadows over the scene.

Judah, the Andersons' girl, was making pancakes. I sat on the lower step and watched, unseen for a moment. And then the ever and all-seeing Quantrill spotted me and nudged Seth, who got up and came over.

"Go back to bed," he said.

"I want to eat with you all."

"We're going soon."

"Then I want to say good-bye."

"I thought we did that yesterday on our ride."

"Are you going to kiss Martha good-bye?"

"Checking up on me, is that it?"

"I think you should take her out on the porch and kiss her. I think she needs it."

"And what do you need?"

My eyes swam with tears. "For you to tell me I'm a wonderful little sister and you love me."

He touched the side of my face. "Course I do. Would I put up with you all these years if I didn't?"

I reached up and put my arms around him and kissed him. He had a stubble of beard on his face. "You didn't shave."

"Didn't have time. Look, Sue Mundy isn't coming along on this trip. She's here to protect you girls in case the Yankees come."

"As a girl or as a man?"

"Does it matter? She's a good shot as either one."

"I like her better as a woman," I told him.

"I've spoken to Martha. You're not to be a pest to Sue. You're not to spend too much time with her. You're to help out around here and do as Martha says. And do your schoolwork. Now I've given Martha money for your keep and to buy fabric for new dresses for you in town. Fall's coming. Think of warm clothes."

"Oh, thank you, Seth. You're the best brother."

He kissed me and, listening to my advice, when they all went outside, he did take Martha aside on the porch to talk. And when they were alone, he kissed her. I know I shouldn't have been watching, but I did. Oh, he was a fine kisser. I wondered where he'd learned all that.

"You oughta be spanked, watchin' your brother like that." It was Judah. She'd come to clear the table. "Bad girl. You want me to tell him?"

"No, please, I . . . just . . . have a special interest. I told him to kiss her good-bye, and I just want to make sure he did it, is all."

"You doan have to make sure that brother of yours knows how to kiss, missy. He sure do from what I seen. Now come on. You might as well sit down an' have breakfast. We goin' to town today."

IT WAS that very day that I found out the shocking truth about Sue Mundy.

I'll never forget the way she told me. It was the first time I felt really betrayed in my life. And the feeling made me sick inside.

I'd been standing aside in the grape arbor after we got back from town, a safe distance from Sue Mundy who was practicing her shooting. She was dressed in her Confederate uniform, right down to the double row of brass buttons in front, with her sash around her waist and shined boots, her hair tucked under her hat, looking very dashing.

She hit the target nearly every time.

She had stopped to reload her pistol when I said to myself: "All these years I've worshipped her, and here she is within feet of me. I ought to do something, say something, and stop acting like a jackass in the rain." True, I'd been in her company all week, but never alone. Always there had been someone else along. And always I'd wanted to say something to her.

Always I'd sensed that she knew it.

I could almost see what there was about her that attracted my brother. She had an aura of confidence, a swagger, a sauciness that Martha did not have.

She stopped shooting just then, holstered her pistol, and waved me over. I went.

"Well," she said, "I'm beginning to think I have a shadow. What did you think of my shooting?"

"You're good," I said.

"But not as good as your brother, hey?"

I didn't answer. Seth never missed his target.

"You know what they tell me about you?" she asked.

My heart thumped inside. "What?"

"That you have a scrapbook about me. Is that true?"

I blushed and looked at the ground. "I had one. For a long time. But it burned when the Yankees fired our house."

"I'll bet it was a beauty," she said.

I nodded yes.

"Hey," and she touched my shoulder briefly, "you goin' shy on me? Don't be shy. It's all a waste of time. I also hear that you can be quite a lively little piece when you want to. Give that brother of yours a run for his money. Good. Keep him on his toes. Wish I could be around when you get older and see how this thing plays out."

"What thing?"

"Never mind. I've something I want you to do for me. Will you listen?"

I nodded yes.

"Come over here, by this tree, and let's sit down."

She took out a cheroot and lighted it, blew out the match, sucked in the smoke, and blew that out, too, then waved it away. Oh, how I wished I could do that! It made you look so grown-up!

She looked amused. "Wanna try?" She took the cheroot out of her mouth and offered it to me.

I didn't want to be a Miss Prissy Boots, but neither did I want to provoke Seth into killing me. "No thanks," I said. "Seth would have kittens if he found out."

"How will he find out?"

"He finds out everything sooner or later."

"I wish I knew that to be true," she said wistfully.

She was sad. Something was bothering her. I waited until she spoke again.

Finally she did. "Your brother," she said carefully, "is smitten with me. At least he thinks he is. What are we going to do about that?"

"I don't know," I said.

"You're taken with me, too, aren't you?"

I blushed down to my toes. "I admire you tremendously," I said decorously.

"It's more than admiration, honey. It's love. Puppy love."

I opened my mouth to object, but she shook her

head no. "Before you go thinking that I'm peculiar, let me tell you why you're in love with me. And what it is that we have to tell your brother."

She paused only a moment, then sighed. "Juliet, I'm not a woman. I'm a man."

Her face wavered in front of me. The words echoed inside my head. "What?"

"You heard me, honey. I'm a man. And you are completely normal. That's why you're in love with me."

I scrambled to my feet. "You're not. You can't be. I've seen you in women's clothes!"

"Clothes don't make the person, Juliet. You see, when I fight alongside the men, I really *am* the Lieutenant Flowers I pretend to be. They all love me for it. They all think I'm a brave, incorrigible woman. The kind of woman they'd marry if they had the courage. And your brother has taken to flirting with me like a schoolboy. He's hooked like a fish on the line, honey. At first I thought it was all great fun, and I planned to tell him one day in the future, and then I come here and I meet Martha."

She hesitated. She inhaled the cigarette. "That sweet, patient, beautiful woman who waits for him to make up his confused mind. And I say to myself: 'Lieutenant Flowers,' I say, 'you can't let this go on. You've got to tell him.' Only I don't because I don't have the courage. And then I meet you."

I said nothing while I tried to piece it all in my head. She was lying, as sure as my name was Juliet. "I don't believe a word of it," I said.

"Why would I make such a thing up?"

"Why not? Look what you've made up already. You've done so much lying you don't know what the truth is anymore."

"Honey, if you were my little sister, I'd slap you for talking like that to me. But instead I'm going to prove I'm not lying another way." And she stood up then and grabbed me by the shoulders and drew me to her. "This," she said, "will open your eyes to a lot of things." And she leaned down and kissed me.

I'd never been kissed like that before. It was at first horrible and intrusive, and then sweet and gentle, and I knew no woman could kiss like that.

Sue Mundy was a man!

He released me and I was wobbly on my feet.

"Who *are* you!" I demanded. "You have no *right*!"

"Darling, sweet girl, I just touched you with a kiss and made you grow up, didn't I?"

"You're a man! You're Lieutenant Flowers!"

"Yes, but that wasn't Lieutenant Flowers kissing you. That was Marcellus Jerome Clark."

"Who is that?"

"My own real name. Juliet Bradshaw, we all have our own private moon. And every moon has a dark side. Only we never dare confront it or let others know about it. Most times we don't even know it is there. Not our moon. Our moon has no dark side."

"What is all this talk about moons? I'm going to tell Seth you kissed me. And then you'll be sorry."

"Ah, Seth. He's what this is all about. Think of what a kettle of fish we're all in here. You and your brother both in love with the same person. Only you're in love with Lieutenant Flowers, and he's in love with Sue Mundy. And then there's poor dear Martha, having to wait for the man she loves, disappointed once already, and she's paying the price. I tell you, Juliet, you have to tell Seth I'm a man. You're the one to do it. And that's what all this is about."

"Me? Why me? Why not you?"

"Because he loves you, sweetie. He's a good, gentle man and he doesn't deserve to suffer, and I know you don't want to see him suffer or be embarrassed, or lose Martha. He'll accept it from you, his darling little sister, more than from anybody else. Please, let's not let this go any further. Will you do this for all of us?"

"So you're going to let your secret out, then?"

"No. That's another thing. You and Seth must never let it out. My disguise is important to Quantrill and the Confederate army. I can't tell you why now, but I will soon. Will you cooperate in this?"

I was privy, mayhap, to confidential intelligence. And I was trapped. My eyes misted over. I had a headache of a sudden. My innards hurt. I stumbled toward the house as if running out of a nightmare.

Chapter Seven

I s it possible that being the possessor of another person's terrible secret can get you so filled up with agony that you can get sick inside? That it can make you *bleed*?

The secret took refuge in my head and my guts. The headache hurt so much that Martha had to give me a cold pack and rub my forehead with vinegar and declare, in her storybook voice, that "a good supper will make you feel better."

I ate. It *was* a good supper. Browned beef and fried potatoes and fresh green beans. I ate in spite of the fact that someone had a fist around my innards and was squeezing the life out of them.

"To bed," Martha ordered. I did not disobey her. She was known to slap one of her sisters if they disobeyed. She stood for no back talk, and I figured she'd not hesitate at slapping me. After all, Seth had left her in charge. I went upstairs, and when I went to put on my nightdress I found blood in my pantalets and panicked, forgetting everything Jenny had told me about becoming a woman. I called out and not only Martha but Jenny came running.

"Too soon," Jenny pronounced solemnly. "I didn't get mine until I was thirteen."

Martha hushed her and ordered her from the room. Then she took it upon herself to give me the most important talk of my life, telling me how to care for myself and where everything was kept.

I fell asleep, both proud and scared, wondering how much Sue Mundy's secret had to do with my getting my monthly of a sudden, and grateful to have a big sister like Martha. *I must get Seth to marry her,* I told myself. Sue Mundy was right. I must speak to Seth, first chance I got.

Sue Mundy came into my room to visit and I threw her/him out. I didn't want a freak around me at the moment when I was about to be welcomed into the legion of womanhood. Martha said I was rude and I said I didn't care. She said she was going to tell Seth and I said I didn't care about that, either.

She said I needn't think because I got my monthly I was out of Seth's jurisdiction. I said I wasn't a little girl anymore. Martha said she still wanted to spank Jenny on occasion. I told her Seth never put a hand on me. Oh, I was a brat, and I had to tell her later that I was sorry.

Then Seth and Bill Anderson and two other Quantrill Raiders arrived home unexpectedly. They returned to remove all the gunpowder and cartridges and guns from the cellar, in case the Yankees came by to confiscate them and blamed us girls for keeping an arsenal in our house.

Box by box, they carried them up the cellar stairs, through the outside entrance, and buried them down by the stream. Then, after they'd washed up and had some food, Seth came up to see me.

"What happened?" He stood by my bed where I was propped up against half a dozen pillows.

"I'm sick."

"With what? I don't need you sick now. You have to be well enough to skedaddle with the others if the Yankees come."

I didn't answer. For heaven's sake, hadn't Martha told him what was ailing me? Well, I wasn't about to tell. Let him guess. He was the expert on women. Do him good to worry a bit.

"I will have an answer," he said. "I have to leave in an hour. Don't send me back with an uneasy mind."

I just looked at him, one of those looks I used to give him when I was very small and he was being very dense. He closed his eyes and shook his head as if to clear it.

"Oh," he said. "Oh, I'm sorry for being such a mulehead. And because Mama isn't here to see you through this."

"I have Martha," I said. "She's been good to me."

"Yes," he said, "but there's more to tell, isn't there? Martha said you were by the barn with Sue Mundy and ran in crying. What was that all about?"

I lowered my head.

"Martha said Sue Mundy kissed you. Or was it Lieutenant Flowers?"

Here it comes, I thought. "Neither," I said.

"Don't lie. You know I can take anything but your lying. Whomever she was pretending to be, nobody has a right to kiss you like that, and I'm going to have a word with her."

"Like what?" I pushed.

"Like what Martha told me she saw. I'll have nobody fooling around with you that way. She'll answer to me."

"I'm not lying, Seth. The man who kissed me was Marcellus Jerome Clark."

"Who in purple hell is that?"

"Sue Mundy. She isn't a girl. She's a man. And she wants me to tell you that."

"Look, Juliet, just because the papers print such claptrap is no reason for you to believe it. Sue Mundy is enough of a girl for any of the men in our regiment."

"Then they're all pansies."

"Now listen here, young lady."

"No, you listen, Seth, please. I have to tell you this. Sue Mundy asked me to. She wants you to know she's not a girl. She's really a man masquerading as a girl."

"Hogwash."

"She knows you flirt with her. And now that she's met Martha she wants to bring a stop to it. Please, Seth. For all your sowing your wild oats, don't let her think you don't know a girl from a man to begin with."

"That's enough, young lady."

I looked at him slyly. "If that's true, then you don't deserve Martha."

I tell you, I wouldn't have blamed him one little bit if he slapped me then. I deserved it. But he didn't. He gripped the bedpost with one hand and his face went hard. "There's a line somewhere here," he said quietly, "and you've just crossed it. And you'll find out how serious that is when you're up and about."

"I'm sorry, but I'm telling you the truth. I knew you wouldn't believe me. So did Sue Mundy."

"Sue Mundy is a damned good soldier."

"I don't care." I started to cry and grabbed a pillow to hug.

Seth moved with a clatter, knocking over a chair. "Enough," he said sternly. "We'll not speak of this. And when you're well and I'm home again, we'll have a long talk about your behavior."

"She's a man," I said again into the pillow. "And you're in love with her. I'm trying to help you. Because there's Martha in love with you, and you don't even care."

He just stood there in that black hat of his, hands on his hips, trying to figure out what to do with me. Clearly he was in a quandary. He was mad, there was no question of it. He wanted to drag me out of bed and hang me on the clothes peg on the door, I suspected. He wanted to take off his wide belt and beat me, only it had four revolvers in it. Or maybe he wanted to build a closet in Martha's basement and put me inside.

So he did the only thing he could. "It's clear this is all a mistake with us," he said quietly. "I'm beginning to be sorry you're my sister. And that orphanage in Kansas City is starting to look more and more appealing to me as the days go by."

He started to leave, then turned at the door. "You stay clear of me for a while. For a while *I don't want anything to do with you.*"

"Seth." I reached out an arm appealingly.

He turned, saying, "I need some time to think things through about us."

Then he walked out. He went back to Quantrill.

Within four days the Yankees came to arrest all of us in the Anderson house.

THEY RODE up in a cloud of dust and dismounted. Their blue uniforms were spotless, the brass buttons shining, the horses sleek and well fed with USA embroidered in gold on the saddle blankets, but still not equal to the blooded horses Quantrill and his men rode. Those horses were from superior stock.

For one clear moment those Yankees seemed to say it

all for me, only I could not decide what it was that they were saying. They touched some chord inside me, some momentary streak of belonging. Then it vanished.

They stood taking measure of the place for a moment or two, conferring. Then a couple of them came up the steps of the porch where I was standing next to Martha. "Ma'am," one said to Martha, "we have to search the premises."

Martha told them to go ahead and search to their heart's content.

As soon as they went in the door, the other girls came out. Jenny, Mary, and Fanny had slept late this morning. Martha and I had enjoyed breakfast in the dining room alone.

As soon as all the girls were in one place the man in charge, Captain Williams, read some kind of a writ saying we were all under arrest "being kin to Quantrill's Raiders and therefore considered persons as had helped the enemy, furnished him with ammunition, and fed and clothed him and given him board."

"Do you see any ammunition in this house?" Martha asked. Oh, she was brave, far more brave than Sue Mundy who'd come to stand with us.

They'd taken all our names. "Kin to Bill Anderson,"

Williams had marked down of the Anderson girls, then looked at me. "And you?"

I had trouble saying it. Maybe Seth said I should stay clear of him, not bother him at all. I hated to connect him with this, then, but I said it, anyway. "I'm sister to Seth Bradshaw," I said.

"Tough cookie," he said of Seth. "And you?" he asked Sue Mundy.

"Sue Mundy," she said quietly.

"Well, never in all my born days," Williams said. And he took off his hat, bowed, then took Sue Mundy's hand and kissed it. "I am honored, ma'am, even as I must arrest you. Gentlemen, look who we have here. A real prize."

"You tell them I'm a man, and I'll tell them where your brother is today," Sue whispered to me later.

"Loyal guerrilla you are."

"I was left to protect you girls. I can only do it if I'm in prison with you."

"Protect the others. Leave me alone."

"No talking!" one of the Yankees barked.

We rode off. To prison.

Chapter Eight

IT WAS a long, hot, and dusty ride, and the man whom I rode behind had no consideration for the bumpiness of the road. He exchanged ribald jokes with another corporal until Captain Williams overheard them and yelled, "No cussing, no dirty joking!" and then all went quiet.

So quiet that I almost fell asleep, rocking back and forth. Once I caught myself leaning my forehead against the back of my corporal, whose name I never did learn, on the edge of sleep enough to catch glimpses of dreams involving Seth. Seth would not know where I was. Likely he would not care. I grew sad and then I was jerked awake again.

THE BUILDING was brick and three stories high, a sad-looking affair that had seen better days. Captain Williams handed a note to one of the superior officers and he read it and glanced at us.

"Blood kin to Quantrill's boys, hey?" he asked. I heard a kind of vicious joy in his voice. "Well, we'll have to treat them like blood-kin, then. Inside, ladies, inside. Take orders and keep your mouths shut and everything'll be all right. We've got some more like you inside."

We were ushered from a hot street into a sweltering building, then led up the rickety stairs to the second floor, where the floorboards were cracked and just as rickety.

The soldier had been right. There were at least twelve more girls and young women in the large room on the second floor, sitting around despairingly. They got up when we came in and stood staring at us—though some of them knew us and we knew some of them.

I knew Armenia Crawford, Chloe Fletcher, Eugenia Gregg, and Lucy Younger from school. Martha took tea, made quilts, and later made guerrilla shirts with some of the older ones. All of them looked unkempt, even to their mussed hair and dirty faces. But more than that, their faces looked white and drawn, their eyes were sunken in, some red from crying.

"How long have you all been here?" Martha asked.

"Three weeks," Chloe Fletcher answered. She seemed to be the spokesperson for them. She stepped forward and took Martha's hand. "We're certainly glad to see you all." She introduced her other girls. Their brothers, like mine, rode with Quantrill.

Martha introduced us and we sat down on the beds, which were lined up against the walls. "And this is Sue Mundy," she finished. "You all have heard of her. She rides with Quantrill."

There were instant *ooh*s and *aah*s. One girl, who'd been introduced as Charity McCorkle Kerr, held close a rag doll, yet she was older than I. She stared at Sue Mundy, unashamedly. "It's right nice of you to come and see us, but we don't have any tea or truffles to offer. You'll have to go elsewhere for that. Oh yes, where did you get the fancy duds?" she asked. "Just you wait. You'll look like the rest of us in no time."

"Charity, dear," Chloe Fletcher interrupted, "we're all in the same boat. I'm sure Sue Mundy is in even greater danger than the rest of us, being she actually fought the Yankees. So leave her alone. Please, darling."

She spoke as if Charity were a little girl. But in the next moment I found out Charity was the wife of one of Quantrill's men. Kerr was her marriage name. And there was a wedding band on her finger.

Charity had reverted in her mind, these last three weeks, to a child. One girl standing behind Chloe Fletcher put her finger to her temple and pointed to Charity and twirled that finger around.

"I can make a sound like a piano," Charity told us, "without assistance of any instrument. I drive the Yankees to distraction at night. I'll play for you all later."

"Go back to your corner now, sweetheart," Chloe directed. And Charity did. She sat down on the floor in a far corner, humming to herself and to her doll baby.

"Poor dear," Chloe whispered. "Her mind is completely gone." She gave a deep sigh. "And I'm afraid of what her husband, Johnny Kerr, will do, when he finds out."

"Will he find out?" I asked boldly. "I mean, will we all ever see our kin again?"

"Have they tried to force themselves on any of you?" Jenny Anderson asked.

"Do they speak of keeping us here? Or sending us somewhere else?" asked Fanny Anderson.

Sue Mundy had been quiet. Finally she spoke. "More to the point, have they questioned any of you?"

Silence. Only Sue Mundy would ask such a pertinent question.

"Some," Chloe answered. Behind her a few hands went up and we heard some yeses.

"Chloe," Sue asked, "do you mind if I have a session with your girls and ask what they've been questioned about? And advise them how to talk to the Yankees in the future?"

Chloe was taken aback, but she said, "Of course." And immediately Sue Mundy ushered the girls to one side of the room and had them sit on the floor as she stood in front of them.

"Go," Martha directed me.

"Do I have to?" I was angry at Sue Mundy and she knew it.

"Yes. This could help you. Seth is a captain now. Directly under Quantrill. They likely know this and will want to question you. Go."

I went and sat down.

The girls who had been questioned by the Yankees were telling Sue Mundy what the tone of the questions had been.

"They wanted to know when my brother was coming home again," said Eugenia Gregg.

"They wanted me to tell them if we had any ammunition around the house, and if I made any cartridges for my brother," stated a girl whom I did not know.

"Does your brother ever tell you about the next raid?" put in Lucy Younger. Then she laughed. "I wouldn't ask. Besides, he wouldn't tell. For my own protection."

It went on like that. Then Sue told them what to say if questioned again by the Yankees. "'I don't know anything. My brother—husband—cousin—said it was for my own protection.' And don't let them threaten you. They can't shoot you as a traitor. The army doesn't make war on women."

Nobody thanked Sue Mundy when she was finished. As a matter of fact, the girls seemed to resent her. Armenia Crawford came over to me. "Who does she think she is in those fancy clothes? She hasn't been sat down across from a dirty-dog Yankee and sneered at and threatened and scared out of her wits. How dare she tell us what to do?"

"The Yankees admire her," I said. "When they came to the house to get us, they were delighted to meet her. The captain even kissed her hand."

She stood stock-still. "Just because she dresses up like a man and shoots them?"

"I guess so."

"There's got to be more to it than that."

"What?"

"I don't know. Let me sleep on it. If I ever sleep in this godforsaken place. Oh, another session this night yet. Now our Chloe is going to give you all the two-cent tour of the place. You better go listen. I wouldn't miss it for the world."

"THE ONLY large windows to let in air are in front," Chloe pointed out. "The side and back of the building have the smaller windows that look out onto weed-choked lots. There is no crosscurrent of air and that's why the place gets stifling hot. As you can see the bunks are set along the other three walls.

"You empty your own slop jars," she went on, to the groans of Jenny and Fanny and Mary, Martha, and even Sue Mundy. "Just throw the contents out the side or back windows. The hogs are waiting below.

"And to change the subject, remember there are guards at the entrance to the building, down on the street, and more at the second-floor landing. The Yankees have a meeting room just outside this room. The walls are thin. So we must be careful of our chatter."

She looked into our fearful faces. "Our girls get so hot during the day they like to take off their dresses and walk around in their shimmies. I can't blame them. Just be careful to carry a shawl or something in case a Yankee comes in. They like to leer at us. They've been away from women a long time, and we don't want to tempt them. Now the food is bad, and it sometimes isn't enough. But eat it if you can. You all have to survive. Thank you."

THAT FIRST night, after a watery dinner of beans and old corn bread, a man came around who was known as Leonard Richardson. He wore an eye patch. Word soon went around the room in a buzz that he was a supplier to wagon train companies.

"I hope he doesn't supply them with this," said Charity McCorkle Kerr. "This food is poison!"

Mr. Richardson gave a short smile as he glanced around the room at the girls seated on the floor. "I represent the town fathers," he told us. "I want to make sure your needs are met."

Always spotless, Martha Anderson stood up then. But I could see her blouse was already stained with sweat, her hair disheveled. "Our needs!" she said. "Sir, we need clean bed ticking, better food, and clean water. Do you know they bring us our water in the slop jars and expect us to drink it?"

"I'll see what I can do about it. Your name is Anderson, isn't it?"

"What difference does it make? I speak for us all."

"We hear your brother, Bill, has offered ten Union prisoners for you and your sisters, that's what difference it makes."

A murmur of *ooh*s and *aah*s went through the room. I sighed. *My brother doesn't even want me for a sister anymore,* I thought.

Then Leonard Richardson looked around. "Who is Juliet Bradshaw?"

Uncertainly, I raised my hand.

"Your brother, Seth, offered five prisoners for your freedom."

A flood of disbelief and gladness rushed through me, even while tears came to my eyes. *Your brother, Seth, offered five prisoners for your freedom.* So he still considered me his sister. He hadn't meant it when he said to stay clear of him, that he didn't want anything to do with me. And all that talk about the orphanage looking good to him? He hadn't meant it after all. *Oh, Seth, I didn't mean to hurt you. I didn't!*

"So what happens now?" I was brave enough to ask.

"It depends on how the Yankees accept the offer. But they're both generous gestures. You girls sure are lucky."

Then another thought came to me. *How did Seth know we were here?* I put the question to Richardson, who only gave that small smile of his. "There's not much Quantrill doesn't know," he told us. "He's got spies." And he shifted his eyes over to a nearby window where Sue Mundy stood smoking a cheroot. "Settle down now. I'll have some clean water sent up."

I set my supper aside. I'd go hungry before I'd eat it.

Chapter Nine

THAT NIGHT, as Charity McCorkle Kerr promised, she played the piano, indeed, without assistance from any instrument. In the summer darkness and with thunder rumbling low in the sky, she played such songs as "Just Before the Battle, Mother" and "Home, Sweet Home." When she started in on "Amazing Grace," some of the girls started to cry, and Chloe Fletcher had to tell her it was enough. So she fell silent, and then we were treated to the sound of her own quiet sobbing and the scratching of rats and other vermin as they ran across the floor.

"Don't bother them and they won't bother us," Chloe directed.

But never, in a hundred years, could I get used to rats under my bed.

Although all the other girls took off their outer clothing, Sue Mundy never did. And because I lay awake long after the others were tossing and turning, snoring and whimpering, I saw her get up and creep across the floorboards and go into the Yankees' room next door. They were all awake in there, and I heard them welcome her.

What was she doing? Did she know them? I sat up but couldn't hear.

"What's she doing in there?" It was Jenny Anderson, whose bed was next to mine.

"I don't know."

"I have a bad feeling about her," Jenny said softly.

"Why?"

"I don't know. Why is she so friendly with the Yankees?"

"Go back to sleep!" Martha Anderson ordered sharply.

I fell asleep before Sue Mundy came back out. And the next morning I awoke about starved. I could not recollect ever being hungry in my life. Besides good food being spread on our table at home, there were always plenty of snacks on the sideboard in the way of nuts and fresh fruit and cake and pie.

Now I understood what the absence of these foods meant. Hunger. Hunger in its worst I-have-a-headache-and-a-pounding-stomachache form. The food the Yankees gave us was no better than what we'd given our pigs at home. It made me want to throw up.

To add to all this, as the day went by the girls decided they wanted to play a game. They wanted each of us to remember some favorite thing from home and tell everyone about it. And so we did.

"I'm thinking of fruit from our trees," said Eugenia Gregg.

"Preserves, especially jelly, from our garden," said Lucy Younger.

"Fresh beans and corn, just picked," said a girl by the name of Trish Taylor.

"Just-made coffee, poured into a cup," added Chloe Fletcher.

"Waffles with powdered sugar on them," said Mary Anderson.

"I remember my cherry chiffonier," I said, changing the subject from food, "with the little round mirror on top. And my cherry washstand with the washbowl of white china. Maxine would have hot water in it for me to wash, every morning."

Charity McCorkle Kerr started to cry softly. "I remember how my husband, Johnny, let me watch when Louie, his personal man, shaved him. I used to love to watch. I wonder if Johnny shaves now." The crying became sobbing then, and Chloe Fletcher said we should stop. So we did.

WITHIN TWO days that second-story room became a hell-hole. My brother, Seth, always said he does not believe in hell, that hell is here on earth, in certain places and in certain people. It certainly was in that second-story room of that prison on Grand Avenue.

We girls got just enough clean water to drink. No more. None to wash in. The days and nights were stifling hot. Except for talking about home we had nothing to do but sit around on the floor or stare out the front windows and watch the people walk by.

The place attracted mosquitoes and flies as well as vermin. And it was the year of the cicadas. The trees were full of them, and the echo of their shrill sound resounded through the nights and days until I thought I would go mad.

Our clothing became dirty and ripped and ragged. Sooner or later we tore off part of our petticoats to wipe our faces of sweat. We took off our shoes and walked about in stocking feet, or better yet, in no stockings at all.

I began to know all the girls' idiosyncrasies.

Amanda Selvey could not tolerate the food at all and threw up all over herself.

Sue Vandiver cried all the time. If Charity McCorkle Kerr started, then so did she, and we couldn't stop them.

Constance Moore was twelve, like me, but she looked and acted sixteen. She had real hefty bosoms and curled up her hair in rags every night as if she were going someplace the next day. She fussed with that hair all the time. I longed to take a scissor and cut it off. She had a book she was reading, and one time when she left it on the floor, unattended, I caught the title of it. *Moll Flanders.* I'd wanted that book when we went into town. I'd asked Seth if I could buy it and he'd said no.

SUE MUNDY constantly visited the Yankees in their room. And we soon learned why: for meals, for washing, for having her dresses laundered by their servant. The Yankees couldn't get enough of talking to her. One of them was taking notes for a book he was writing on her, he said. I felt sorry for him. Sue Mundy was telling him all lies.

Juliette Wilson, whose brother rode with Dick Yeager, had a talent like Charity McCorkle Kerr, only hers involved a guitar. She pretended she was strumming one and with her tongue and palate she could sound so like one that it frightened everybody. The Yankees made her stop every time they heard it.

By the third day, I had been approached by at least three or four girls about Sue Mundy's friendliness with the Yankees.

"Why do they like her?" wondered Fanny Anderson.

"Is she a spy?" asked Chloe Fletcher. "We were told she is one for Quantrill. But do you suppose she's a double agent, spying for the Yankees, too?"

The questions came down on me fast and furious, since my brother fought beside her. I had to tell them I didn't know. Because I didn't. Though I did remember what Sue Mundy had told me the day she revealed her true sex to me.

My disguise is important to Quantrill and the Confederate army. I can't tell you why now, but I will soon.

———

THOUGH EVERYONE said Jenny Anderson and I looked alike, Jenny had beautiful brown curls. One of the guards who came in every day to check on things was Arnold Rucker. He looked to be about seventeen, but he was raw, untamed. And he started making passes at Jenny.

She wouldn't abide it. First she slapped him. Then he grabbed her and attempted to kiss her. Martha tried to intervene, but he pushed Martha aside and she lost her balance and fell backward. Jenny, angered, kicked him in the groin, and he yelled and crumpled to the floor. A second guard came in, a brutish-looking fellow, who cussed and ordered our drinking water taken from us, then demanded that a twelve-pound ball and chain be put around Jenny's ankle for punishment.

Martha argued. "She's my little sister. I strongly object."

"Object all you want to, lady," said the brutish-looking fellow. "Rules are rules. And I can't have her kicking my men."

"But what about what he did to her? And to me? We want Leonard Richardson. He's our intermediary."

"He's not here today."

"We demand to see him. It's our right."

The man laughed. "You don't get it, do you, lady. You got no rights. This ain't no democracy. You gave up all that stuff when you quit the Union, and Jeff Davis is far away. Now shut your mouth. We got more balls and chains."

What hurt Martha most was being spoken to such-like. Never in her life had she had to endure such rudeness. She went and sat down in a far corner to hide her tears, and I sought her out. I knelt on the floor in front of her. She was a big sister to me.

"I'm sorry the brute spoke to you so," I told her. "If Seth were here that brute would be picking himself up off the floor."

She sniffed into her handkerchief. "I'm ashamed to let you see me cry. I wanted so to be strong for you all. You won't tell Seth I cried, will you?"

I shook my head. "We've all got secrets to keep," I said. "I only wish I knew where Seth and the others were."

Now she shook her head. "Nearby," she whispered. "But I won't tell you. The less you know, the more you're out of danger."

"How do you know?"

"Sue Mundy. She found out from the Yankees."

"Martha, everybody is saying she's a double agent. Is she?"

"I don't know, Juliet. But she finds information out from them, whatever you call her."

"Well, if they know, why don't they attack Quantrill and his men?"

"Because they move around too fast. They can never be found. All the Yankees know is that they're in the area. They spy on each other, the two groups. And Sue Mundy is right in the middle."

"Martha," I said, giving the conversation a new turn, "you should know, my brother doesn't love her. He's never kissed her. He wanted me to tell you that. He loves you."

She smiled through her tears. "I know."

"You know?"

"Of course. A woman always knows."

"Are you going to marry him?"

"If he ever comes to his senses, yes."

"Oh, Martha." I grabbed her hand. "You'll be my real sister then."

She dried her eyes. "He loves you, too," she said. "Don't let all his strutting and spitting out hard words frighten you. When it comes down to it, he's soft on the inside. He just doesn't know how to show it, is all."

I went to bed that night with a warm glow inside me. You would never know the cicadas were screaming outside and the girls crying inside, and those who weren't crying were whimpering and restless. It's funny what knowing you are loved can do. Too bad it didn't last long.

Chapter Ten

EVERY FEW minutes, Jenny Anderson tried to turn over in her bunk, could not for the ball and chain, and whimpered heartbreakingly. Martha stayed beside her, soothing her with words. Sue Mundy had gone into the Yankees' room to beg forgiveness for Jenny and ask that the contraption be taken off, at least for the night.

"I'll sign all the memo pads or pieces of paper you want," she promised. For they all wanted her signature. But this time her magic did not work. And she came out of the Yankee headquarters disheartened. She circulated from girl to girl that night, saying a few words to each one to comfort them.

I thought it was decent of her not to try to squeeze into the bunks with the girls. After all, when all was said and done, she was still a man.

Finally she made her way over to me. "Don't you come near me, you gypsy, you," I told her/him. "Shame on you, here in a room full of half-dressed women who all need baths. And you prettified up as for a ball. How do you get those Yankees to wash and clean your clothing?"

"They are thrilled by me and my exploits," Sue Mundy said. "They all can't wait to go home and tell their relatives that they met me. My name is currency, in the North as well as the South. Many of them will have dinners bought for them at inns with the promise to tell that they met me."

"I wouldn't let anybody trade on my name," I said.

"Half the soldiers fighting in this war are trading on the names of those whom they've met, and flashing souvenirs. It happens in all wars," she said.

"You. You're a spy. Else why would you be here?"

"I told you once. Yes, I spy for him."

I shrugged. "Well, your big report tonight can be that Jenny Anderson has a ball and chain tied around her ankle. Twelve pounds it weighs. And don't you dare say she deserves it or I'll hit you over the head with something. Just don't you sleep near me. Go somewhere else. You don't know the trouble you got me into with my brother."

Jenny Anderson whimpered pitifully. I could see the form of Martha putting a pillow under Jenny's ankle to try to make it more comfortable.

While Martha was doing this, the ball rolled off Jenny's bunk and slammed onto the wooden floor, making an earsplitting sound.

The Yankees must have thought Quantrill and all his raiders were attacking. They burst through the door from their private quarters in various modes of undress, some without shirts, some without boots, some in their Skivvies, but all with guns.

"What in the name of purple hell is going on here?" the head Yankee roared.

He carried a lantern. It cast shadows all over the place. I wished, like Charity McCorkle Kerr, that I had a rag doll to cling to. She, incidentally, was still in her corner, "playing the piano" for that doll.

The head Yankee looked at her and frowned. "Somebody shut that kid up or I'll shoot her," he threatened.

Martha went over to do so.

I slept fitfully that night, and in the morning when the gruel was handed out, I could not bring myself to eat it, though my stomach rumbled with hunger. Sue Mundy came over with a dish of eggs and bacon and sat down beside me.

"I'd give you some of this if only you'd be friends."

She was bargaining. I was wise enough, taught by Seth, to know that. What did she want? "Always find out what the other person wants first," Seth had taught me. "You'll place him at a disadvantage if you know."

"What is it you want from me?" I asked her.

She laughed softly. "Somebody's schooled you. You'd make a good spy. Here, take a piece of bacon and I'll tell you."

I humiliated myself by taking a piece of bacon. A "Judas kiss," Seth called it, though he wasn't much on the Bible.

"All I want to know is where Seth's house is," she said quietly. "And not for me. Or the Yankees. But for you. I think, when all this is over, you should go there for safety. The Yankees are talking of some order being written up, sending the others out of this district. I don't think you should go. Seth is here, and Seth is all you have."

"I know where it is," I said. "Seth took me there. What does it matter to you?"

"It doesn't. I was just making conversation. Look, sweetie. I'm sorry if I hurt you and got you into trouble with Seth. You're a darling girl, and I want to make it up to you. So I'm telling you this: Go to your brother's farm. You can make things up to Seth there. Prove you're no little pest of a girl."

I was about to come back with a sassy reply when the building seemed to tremble. It shook for about three minutes. "An earthquake," Amanda Selvey said.

"No, this place is falling down!" yelled Chloe Fletcher. She was not joking.

I opened my mouth. No words came out. My whole being shook. The walls trembled, and the floor bucked. Some girls were screaming. The door to the Yankees' room blew open and a guard yelled in to us. "Come on. Get out! Now!"

Chapter Eleven

I OPENED MY mouth to say something, but no words came out. I was, for the moment, oddly fascinated with the way the bunks were sliding across the floor. By then the whole building was shuddering and there were grinding and screeching noises coming from the wood and bolts that held it together.

Plaster started falling from the ceiling, hitting some of the girls on the shoulders or heads. I saw blood where it shouldn't be, on blond curls and chestnut braids. Joists and timbers fell with terrible noises. Then came the sound of gunshots.

Gunshots? Were the Yankees attacking now, too? No, those sounds were the walls popping open.

All was confusion. Clothes caught on wood and ripped. Girls fled by me with looks of horror in their eyes. Where were they going?

I looked down to see an object sliding toward me. It was Charity McCorkle Kerr's rag doll. I looked beyond it to see her still in her same corner, playing a lullaby on her piano. I picked up the rag doll and held it close. The floor was rocking back and forth now, the windows coming loose from their frames and falling to the ground, the glass shattering all over the place, the wood splintering.

"Out!" The guards pulled Eugenia Gregg and Lucy Younger out the door and tried to come back for more, but the doorway was blocked by a piece of ceiling that had fallen in the meantime.

"The front windows!" someone yelled. "Jump out the front windows!"

"I'm not leaving without my sister Jenny," Martha Anderson announced, as if people were cajoling her to leave. Her voice no longer reminded me of a fairy tale; it was a voice of determination. She pulled Jenny off her bunk, ball and chain with her, across the floor, which already had cavernous holes in it, to the front windows, where she picked her up.

"Come on, before the roof caves in on us," Sue Mundy said. I hadn't seen her in the last several minutes, hadn't even thought of her. She was from another world already, a world I'd had to put aside. The world of my childhood. And whether she was man or woman—and who was in love with her or not—was no longer of concern. This was the here and now. Buildings falling in. Girls screaming and unable to escape. Knowing they were going to die.

This was the Yankee twenty-cent special on how to grow up fast.

"I can't," I told Sue Mundy. "What about the other girls?"

In answer came a long, drawn-out grinding noise, then dust, thick and in my eyes, wood and bricks falling all over. And then I felt myself being lifted. By a man. And then, of a sudden, flying through the air and landing hard on the street below, then rolling over and over.

Was it Seth? Had he come to rescue me? When I was small, Seth used to hold me in his arms like this and we would roll down the hill at home and I'd scream with the thrill of it.

But this wasn't a grassy hill. There were bricks underneath us, and people standing all around. And there was blood on the side of my face and my head felt as if it had cracked open. I felt like Humpty Dumpty who had fallen off the wall, never to be put together again.

And for some reason I was holding a rag doll like the one I used to own. But the man holding me was not Seth.

It was Marcellus Jerome Clark, strong as Seth and still dressed as Sue Mundy.

In the next instant he was gone, whispering, "Someone will help you." In the minute after that, somebody landed with a dull thud right next to me. I could scarce turn my head to look for the terrible jagged pain. My eyes and ears didn't work so good with the dust settling in them and the screams and shouts of the people assembled all around.

The person who had landed next to me was Martha Anderson, on top of her sister Jenny with the ball and chain. There was a long beam on top of Martha and one end of it had landed on top of me, but I didn't feel it. *Is this what they mean when they say people are in shock?* I wondered.

"Hold on, honey, we'll help you." It was the man with the eye patch, Leonard Richardson.

"They need help more than I do." I pointed at Martha and Jenny, though it hurt to talk.

It took only a few minutes for them to remove the beam and to see that Martha had a gash in her side from landing on the chain. She was crying hysterically because she thought she had killed her sister.

"No," Richardson told her. "That's what killed her."

The twelve-pound ball had gone right through Jenny's body. There was more blood coming out of Martha than any one person had the right to have. Richardson and some others had bandages now and were attempting to stanch it. After they had bound Martha's side, she sat half up and asked for her sisters. "Where's Mary?" she asked. "Where's Fanny?"

"Being taken care of, ma'am," Richardson told her.

But when I looked him in the eye, I could see he was lying. At least one of them was dead.

"Where are you taking her?" I asked. "You must let me know. She's my brother's promised."

"Don't worry, you're going with her." He bandaged

my head, which was badly gashed, and gave me laudanum and water. My left arm was fractured, too. "I'm
known in town as Richardson, but my real name is Jack
Andrews. I'm a spy for Quantrill." He said it quietly.

My head was muddled. I kept going in and out of
consciousness. "Why does everybody have two names?"
I asked. "And why does everybody spy for Quantrill?"

He gave me some kind of an answer, but I could
make no sense of it. They were putting Martha on a
stretcher now, and he explained that they were taking
us to a special ward at the army hospital at Fort
Leavenworth.

"No one will know where to find us," I said, crying
at the same time.

"Remember who you're talking to. Seth will know.
Now be good and brave so I can tell him."

"Seth doesn't love me anymore." Thank heaven that
I was babbling, because he put it down to a fever.

"Tell that to somebody who doesn't know him.
Didn't he offer five Yankees for your release? Come now,
let the potion do its work. Don't fight it."

All I could see now through my tears as they carried
my stretcher to the waiting ambulance were faces peering
down at me and women clucking and shaking their

heads and murmuring, "Why, they're just children. Since when do we Yankees go to war against children?"

"Somebody said most of them got killed when the building fell," a man was saying.

"Dear God," from another man. "There will have to be some investigation into why this building fell. Answers must be had."

They lifted my stretcher into the back of the ambulance. Every turn of it, every bump, sent me into agony. "Martha," I cried, "where is Martha?"

"You're a good girl for looking out for your brother's intended," Jack Andrews said. "We're putting her right beside you. I'm riding along. And at the hospital I'll make sure you two are together."

"Who's going to tell Seth?"

He winked at me. "It's all been taken care of," he said.

Chapter Twelve

FORT LEAVENWORTH was to the north, they said, but it could have been in heaven for all I knew right then. And I don't know how long it took us to get there. The rocking, horse-drawn ambulance could have been a sweet chariot carrying me home, I was so near unconscious from the laudanum. Next to me on her stretcher, Martha slept and moaned. I reached over and took her hand. I minded that she must be in a very bad state. Would she die? What would Seth do if she did? I knew how smitten he was with her.

With my free hand I hugged Charity McCorkle Kerr's rag doll. Somebody had said Charity was dead. I wondered how many girls had died, and I wondered how I had managed to live.

Sue Mundy, that's how. I hated being beholden to her, but I was.

What with all the rocking and the low talk of the men on horseback outside and my occasional glimpse of the stars in the sky, I fell asleep. I didn't want to do that. Somebody had to stay awake to give them what for if they took us to another prison.

I didn't wake up through all the rest of it, through them carrying us into the hospital and up to the second floor, the floor allotted for "the girls belonging to Quantrill." I slept through the doctor who examined us and fixed our wounds and the sentries who opened the gates in the first place. Sadly, there were only about four other girls besides us who made it.

When I did wake, I saw we were in total darkness, with the exception of one candle burning on a nightstand at the foot of my bed. Someone was talking in a low voice.

"The father will be here in a few minutes."

"We have but a few minutes." Was that Seth's voice? "If the Yankees find us, I'll be hanged. I mustn't be caught. I've too many scores to settle."

"Here comes the father now."

It *was* Seth talking. I could see two, maybe three, and then four forms standing around Martha's and my beds. "Seth," I called out weakly.

He moved toward me. "Juliet, yes. I'm here."

"Is it really you, Seth?"

"Yes, honey. They came and got us. Bill Anderson is here, too."

"Is Martha dying?"

"No. Why do you say such?"

"Why do you need a priest?"

He was holding my hand. I was crying quietly. Tears were coming down my face. With his free hand he wiped them away.

"Seth," I said, "I'm sorry."

"Hush, don't you dare. Sorry has no place here."

"She saved me. Sue Mundy. Jumped out the window holding me." I didn't dare say Marcellus Jerome Clark. Leave it be. Let it die. Let it crumble under the building. "Do you still want me for a sister?"

"I've got you. I'm stuck with you. The Constitution of the United States says I can't give you back."

"I thought you gave all that up, the Constitution."

He leaned over and kissed me. "I need you to do

something for me now. Will you?" His voice was ragged, full of tears.

"What can I do, the way I am?"

"I'm going to marry Martha. Bill Anderson is going to be my best man. Martha and I would like you to be our maid of honor."

"I can't stand up."

"You don't have to. Just be there for us."

The father was putting his priest's long stole around his neck and holding a Bible, though he couldn't see to read. Martha held Seth's hand and the words were said. Low, like the stars outside. Bright like them, too. My own heart was bursting inside me. Those darned tears wouldn't stop flowing down my face.

We weren't Catholic, but the Andersons were, and Seth stood staunch and proud and I don't think wedding vows ever meant so much, especially with him knowing the Yankees could get word that he and Bill were here any minute, and the result could be a hanging tree.

Bill Anderson produced a ring from somewhere. Said it was his mother's, and Seth put it on Martha's finger, then leaned down to kiss her, long and full of his love.

Bill was tugging at his arm. "We gotta go."

"Yes." He came to my bed and kissed me again. "Martha has instructions. Listen to her and behave."

In the next instant it was as if they never were. The room was empty again, and silent, and dark except for the one candle glowing on the nightstand at the foot of my bed.

Chapter Thirteen

"I NEED YOU," Seth was saying softly. It was the second time in a week that he'd said that to me, and I wasn't upset at hearing it.

"What for?"

He was holding a set of brown trousers and a Quantrill shirt in his hands. He set the clothing down on the bed. "I should say Quantrill needs you. I was sent to bring you along to the camp at White Oak."

My heart beat very fast. Was he joking? He was not. He gave the clothes a small push toward me on the bed. "How is the arm? And the head? Do you still have a fever? Are you still as weak as you were, or are you better?"

He sat down on the side of my bed and felt my head. His hand went gently over the bandages and he felt my arm. "Head still hurts, hey?"

I nodded yes. He ran his hand over the healing cuts on my face. There were many of them. "They'll leave scars," I said, "and I won't be pretty anymore."

"They'll heal. We'll ask Maxine for some of her special concoctions. Look, I wouldn't bother you this morning, but this is important. You feeling up to an assignment from Quantrill?"

That was like asking me if I wanted to walk on the moon. "Yes."

He didn't like the whole idea himself, he said, but Quantrill needed someone who had been at the prison, who would be able to tell him what it had been like, how they'd been treated. And besides Martha and a few girls with bad injuries here in the hospital, all were dead.

"I'll do it," I said solemnly.

"And keep your mouth shut? No questions? Of me or anybody? And take these clothes off soon as you're done?"

"Yes."

"Good, put them on." The room was near dark in the morning half-light, but he went over to Martha's bed anyway and sat on the edge of it and stroked her hair away from her forehead. She must have come awake because they spoke in low tones while I struggled to dress.

The boys' clothing was rough against my skin. But I didn't mind. An assignment from Quantrill was all I was thinking. Would he make me a spy like Sue Mundy? Where was Sue Mundy, by the way, and why wasn't she doing this, and what in God's name had ever made my brother agree to allow me to take part in something so outrageous?

He answered some of these questions when we were out in the chilly August morning, mounting our horses. He'd managed to secure a horse for me, and for that I was grateful. But he was a man of few words, and, as promised, I asked no questions.

"We're going to Camp White Oak, where Quantrill is holed up," he explained briefly. "Quantrill is brewing a plan in retribution for so many kin of his men being killed in the prison collapse. Sue Mundy is on another spying mission for him. And we all know she wasn't treated as a prisoner, anyway.

"They're going to vote this morning on Quantrill's next attack," he told me quietly. "After you leave. And depending on what you say. No, you cannot know what it is. Or when. Just tell the truth as I've taught you to tell it. No embellishments. No pretty words. Spare the words, instead. Tell everything you saw, everything everyone said to the Yankees and they to our kin. Be polite and respectful. Then I'll take you back to the hospital and you will never, in all your born days, speak of this morning again. Do you hear?"

"Yes, Seth."

"Good girl. Now silence. We don't have far to go."

About a mile from the camp we stopped so he could put a blindfold on me. "For your own safety," he explained. "Now, if asked, you can honestly say you don't know how to get to this camp."

He led my horse by the reins and I held on to the pommel tightly. Soon, very soon, I heard low talking. Then we stopped again and the talking stopped, too, and he removed the blindfold and gave me back the reins.

At first I was blinded by the morning sun coming through the trees. I heard, rather than saw, the men who knew me saying their greeting.

"Hey there, Juliet, how you doin', kid?"

"See your head is still bandaged up. Does it hurt?"

"You kin put all the boys' clothes on her you want, Seth, she still looks mighty fetchin'."

Low laughter. But respectful.

They all wore the gray Quantrill shirts with the red stitching. Some were cleaning guns, others brushing down horses. Some were eating and some huddled around a campfire sipping coffee.

"Get her some coffee," one of them said. "Where're your manners, boys? We have a lady present. Treat her like one."

It was Quantrill. He'd been leaning against an oak tree smoking a cheroot and talking with Bill Anderson in low tones, and now he came over and looked up at me for a full minute. "How do you feel?" he asked.

"I'm middling well, sir."

He nodded. "You of a mind to tell us a story?"

"Yes, sir."

He nodded. "Get her down, Seth. Bring her over to that tree. Bill, get a blanket and spread it on the grass. Ground's cold. Somebody got coffee and vittles for Juliet Bradshaw?"

Of a sudden the camp came alive. Everyone went to do his bidding. Seth lifted me off my horse and someone led him away for food and water. Seth carried me over to the tree and set me down on the blanket next to Quantrill. For a while it was just me and Quantrill and Seth, eating and drinking the heavenly coffee in the sun-washed morning with the pleasant murmur of the men's talk around us. And the horses munching grass and the fire crackling.

Then, as if given a signal, everything changed. "All right," Quantrill said. "Listen up."

They gathered around with their guns in hand, like children about to hear a bedtime story. The looks on their faces had changed. Now they were weary, bitter, and sad.

"You can ask about your kin as we go along," Quantrill told them. "But I want no cussing. And anybody frightens this here little girl will answer to me. Got it?"

They nodded yes.

And so I began my story, from the first day we got to the three-story brick building at 1409 Grand Avenue. I wished I could speak like Martha, with a storytelling voice that would make them feel as if everything would be all right, but I knew I couldn't do that. Because I knew, and they knew, and likely now even Martha knew that we couldn't count on anything being all right again. Ever.

I told them about the food. The sleeping arrangements. The lack of clean water. The stifling heat. The water given to us at first in slop jars until Martha demanded better.

Sometimes they stopped me to ask a question about a little sister, or a cousin, and how she behaved. Or how she "answered them back" or how she "took all that sass," and always I made their kin stand out in a bright and shining light. Because most of the girls they asked about were dead.

And if I was lying, well, then God would have to deal with me. But I was sure that even He would understand.

I saw Bill Anderson bite his lip as I told how Jenny kicked and fought the Yankee guard and how they put the ball and chain around her ankle. "She would do that," he murmured. "She would."

I even told them how it was when the building shook and trembled, and how Sue Mundy got me out of there. And how we were driven to Fort Leavenworth. And how some of the girls were crippled for good now, but still at Leavenworth. And then I ended with "If there's anything else I can do, Captain Quantrill, I'll do it, sir, gladly."

He gave me a thin smile. But it didn't travel into his eyes. "Thank you, sweetheart, but there is one thing."

"Yes, sir?"

"You can call me colonel."

"Yes, sir, Colonel."

Nobody laughed. He stood up. The men stood up. "We'll take a vote on the matter later this evening," he told them. "You have the truth now about what happened. Mull it over. Meantime, Bradshaw will take his sister back to Leavenworth."

The men dispersed. I looked at Seth.

"They're going to vote on how to retaliate. Hush now, not another word about it. Come on, we've got to get you back."

And so we rode off.

About a mile from the camp, when Seth took the blindfold off me again, he started to speak, very softly.

"You should know," he said, "something about Sue Mundy."

My ears perked up. Was he about to tell me he knew, now, that she was a man?

But no, it was not that. I doubted he would ever talk about that with me, since the subject had almost caused him to give up on me and made me hate him temporarily.

"This information I'm about to give you is as

confidential as the meeting with Quantrill this morning. Hear me?" He was using his stern voice.

"Yes, Seth." I was using my obedient one.

"She's pretending to be a double agent," he said. "Do you know what that is?"

"Yes."

"Tell me."

"It means she spies for the Yankees as well as for us."

"Good girl. Or not so good. I don't know. In other times girls your age were lucky if they could name the Big Dipper in the sky. I don't know if I like the kind of education this war is giving you. But we can't help it, so we might as well be as smart as we can about it before it kills us all. Listen to me now, this is important. She isn't spying for the Yankees. She just lets them *think* she is. That's why they like her so and do special favors for her. Are we clear on all this now?"

"Yes, Seth. But—"

"But what?"

"Some of the girls in the prison were already starting to say that about her. That she was spying for the Yankees, because she was talking with them in secret so much."

"Where are those girls now?"

I bit my lip and lowered my head.

"I don't hear anything," he pushed.

"They're dead, Seth."

He just looked at me. "And those who lived have a lot more on their minds these days. Like learning to walk again. Or see. Or wondering if they're going to live. Don't they?"

"Uh-huh."

"I don't like *uh-huh*s. I like yes or no."

"Yes," I said.

"I'm bullying you," he admitted, "and I promised myself I would never do that again. When I found out that the Yankees took you, I made all kinds of deals with God, that if He let you be all right, I'd be the best brother and guardian in the world to you. I'm not doing so good, am I?"

He stopped his horse, and I stopped mine. "You are the best," I told him.

"Well, if I mess things up and start to bully you, you just tell me, okay? Throw cold water in my face or something. I don't want to be like the old man. God, I don't want to be. You know what I discovered? There are different ways of locking people in closets. Sometimes you can do it without having a closet. But you can still keep that person locked away forever. Do you understand, Juliet?"

"Yes, Seth."

He nodded and we started on. "You mustn't tell anybody what I just told you about Sue Mundy. Few people know it. Quantrill does, of course; I do, and a couple of other captains in the group. If word got out, the Yankees would hang her. And she's good at what she does. She can wrap the Yankees right around her little finger.

"Oh," he said, "and Martha doesn't know. Be careful around Martha. I don't want to involve her in this. But you've been friends with Sue Mundy. So I had to caution you."

And so it was that I became the pivotal one to help Colonel Quantrill and his men decide what move to make to get back at the Yankees for the collapse of the building at 1409 Grand Avenue and the deaths of so many of their kin.

Nobody knows I was there. Likely nobody ever will, except me and Seth, Martha, and the remaining Quantrill Raiders. It's a heavy burden to carry, considering what they did. And sometimes a person needs help carrying it.

Chapter Fourteen

MARTHA WAS still ailing. But the day I got back from Quantrill's camp they had her out of bed and she was practicing walking around with crutches.

That was the nineteenth of August. The stitches held in her side, and she told me the doctor had said the wound lessened her chance of having children.

"I told Seth last night," she said. "He said never mind, we're going to make beautiful children."

Her voice trailed off. I dared not ask more.

"So, I hear you told our story to Quantrill," she said quietly.

I nodded. "Seth told me I'm not to talk about it to anyone."

"Of course. I'm sorry for asking. My, things are getting tangled between all of us, aren't they?" She gave a small smile. She still had that singsong quality to her voice, as if the fairy story was still going to have a happy ending to it after all. "Well, we can talk about where we're going when we get out of here, can't we?"

"Of course."

"Well, Seth wants you and me to go to his house in the holler. He believes it to be the safest place around. Only thing is the Yankees will want to escort us, so we have to lie and say the place belongs to Sue Mundy."

"But that's not fair."

"Nothing in the world is these days, Juliet. If the Yankees knew it was Seth's place, they'd burn it. Just like they did to your home."

I fell silent for a moment, then asked, "When do we go?"

"When the Yankee doctors let us out of here. Certain things have to happen first, I suppose."

The retaliation, I thought. The vengeance from Quantrill and his men. The Yankees knew it was coming, but they didn't know where or when. And until they did know, they were going to keep us all where they could keep an eye on us. Just in case they needed to imprison us again, I supposed.

Martha gave me a look and a weak smile. I smiled back at her. We were likely thinking the same thing, but neither of us would acknowledge it. The worst had happened, we chose to believe. How could the Yankees do anything more to us?

WE WERE still in the hospital at Leavenworth on the twenty-first of August when Quantrill and his men closed in on the well-cared-for little town of Lawrence, Kansas, and attacked.

They expected, all four hundred of them, to be attacked along the way by Yankees. But they weren't.

First they sat on a hillock overlooking the handsome town of some hundred homes that boasted the largest grocery store in the state and the grandest hotel west of the Mississippi.

Then they went into the town like wolves, quietly and stealthily, only one order of Quantrill's ringing in their ears: "I will have no woman harmed."

They came right down Massachusetts Street screaming, "This is for the girls!"

They told us all this later, when they told us that Bill Anderson was the first one in, the first one to fire his gun at a helpless man who'd dropped his to the ground and raised his hands in surrender.

"This one is for Jenny!" Bill yelled. And on he went, with so many more for Jenny.

They killed, they burned, they attacked, they ransacked, they looted. They set fire until Lawrence lay in blackened, burning ruins like the underside of hell.

My brother and the other Quantrill Raiders, I thought, were riding through the dark side of their moons.

MY HEAD still hurt when the doctor changed the bandage before we left the hospital.

"Do I still need a bandage?" I asked him.

"No," he said. "But it'll help, where you're going."

It was August 25. Sue Mundy was there, with me and Martha, having come back from her spy mission, which I suspected had something to do with Lawrence.

"Where are we going?" I asked him. His name was Dr. Powers and he was the one to tell us about Lawrence. He chose no sides, though a Yankee. He treated everyone with kindness and consideration.

"Well, General Order Number 11 came down this morning from headquarters."

"What does that mean?"

"Means all persons from Jackson, Cass, and Bates counties have to remove themselves from their present place of residence. They want to rid the border of all those who may have provided food, housing, clothing, or ammunition for Quantrill's men."

"It means," Sue Mundy put in, "that they couldn't kill all of you when the building fell so they've got to get rid of you another way."

Martha hobbled over on crutches. "It means us, Juliet," she told me. "And we're only allowed to bring the clothes on our backs and what we can carry."

"I have a nightgown on my back," I said, "and so do you."

"Doctor," Martha appealed, "can you get permission somehow for us to make a visit to our house and get some clothes? I know it's a big favor, sir, but we can't go like this."

"I agree with you, Mrs. Bradshaw, and I'll see to it this day. But you're in no condition to do it. Maybe the powers that be will allow Sue Mundy here to fetch some things for you. Why don't you make a list."

Chapter Fifteen

Sue Mundy returned the next day with clothes and sturdy shoes for Martha and me. We were thankful to learn that so far the Anderson home had escaped the Yankees' torch. But Sue Mundy could not sweet-talk the Yankees on another matter.

"The girl and her sister-in-law are both casualties of that dreadful prison crashing to the ground," she told the corporal in charge. "They're going to be having hearings and investigations. This little girl can testify about the whole thing. She's a valuable witness. You oughtn't send her away. And her sister-in-law is a valuable witness, too."

"What do you want me to do with them?" the corporal asked. "Take them home to Mother?"

"No," Sue Mundy answered. "Let me take them to my house and keep them there. I'll stay and keep them under guard."

"Look, I've got my orders," he said. "They go on the caravan, out of state."

"Cass County had ten thousand residents on the day this order came down," a corporal told us. "As of today, only about six hundred remain."

We stood on a little rise on the plains, looking at the strange caravan winding along the narrow dirt trail that led out of Missouri. The caravan was made up of army wagons, oxcarts, even large crates with wheels imposed on them. Some were pulled by oxen, some by mules, some by old horses, and some by people.

Sue Mundy was gone. Back to rejoin Quantrill. The corporal had let her go, which proved what Seth had said to me about her claiming to be a double agent.

"Where are the wagons headed?" Martha asked. "Where will we be headed?"

"Don't know," the corporal said. "North, east, or south in Missouri, anywhere not affected by the proclamation.

To the eastern states. Kansas, Kentucky, Tennessee, or Texas. Anywhere you want."

"But we don't know anyone in those places," I objected. "And our families won't know where we are."

"Don't matter. You brung it on yourselves."

"My brother, Seth. He's the only family I have. I have no one else."

"Then he should have kept a better rein on you than to let you go helping to supply the Raiders with shirts and food and the like."

I ignored that. Who had known it would come to this? "He's Martha's husband," I said. "And she's been hurt. You mean she'll never see him again?"

"If they'd told us they were married so we could keep record, instead of letting us find out through the grapevine, we'd have made other plans for them. And you."

"What is all that smoke on the horizon?" Martha asked.

"Wheat fields," he answered matter-of-factly, "cornfields. Houses and barns. Everything in the area is to be burned. Orders."

"Our home!" Martha cried, and bowed her head, leaning on her crutches.

"Here, ma'am," he said politely, for he was nothing if not polite. "Come along. You and the little girl had better get into this here wagon before you collapse." And he halted a wagon with a woman and a child in it. It was pulled by a young boy.

I still had the mumblefuddles as I climbed into the wagon. That is to say, my head was still dizzy and hurt and sometimes my eyes didn't focus right. But I didn't say anything to Martha. She had enough to spend her energy on.

The woman in the wagon said her name was Catherine. It was her child she was carrying, she told Martha. A boy, about three. A fine-looking boy at first sight, chubby and sleeping in her arms.

It took Martha only two minutes to see that he was dead.

The woman knew. Quiet tears were rolling down her face. "I don't know what to do," she told Martha. "I'll have to bury him. But I don't know where. John, my other son there, will have to dig a grave for me."

"There's an ash tree up ahead," Martha told her. "Will the soldiers let us stop?"

The caravan was being brought along and guarded by Yankee militia.

"They'll have to. Or they can shoot me, too. Does anybody think I care?"

Her son, about fourteen, pulled the wagon under the ash tree and immediately two Yankee soldiers on horseback came over to see what we were about. "You got trouble, ma'am?" one of them asked.

Catherine settled herself under the tree with the little fellow still in her lap as if she were at a garden party. "He needs to be buried," she told them. "Do either of you care to dig his grave?"

"He dead?" one of them asked.

"Well," she answered quietly, "I don't usually bury my children unless they are."

Ashamedly they took small shovels from their supplies on their horses' backs and proceeded to dig, while Catherine held the child close and sobbed quietly. Martha was crying quietly now, too. Tears were coming down my own face.

At first they couldn't get the little fellow out of Catherine's arms. But Martha set her crutches aside and held her while they did, then picked up the crutches, and with one of us on either side we walked away while they put the child in the ground.

When it was over, the soldiers asked Catherine if there was anything they could do for her.

"She needs a decent wagon. And a horse to pull it. Her other son is exhausted," Martha said, speaking up like she did back on Grand Avenue in the prison.

One of them went to find such a vehicle, and the other looked at me and Martha. "Where'd you two get hurt?" he asked.

"We were in the Grand Avenue prison when it fell," I told him.

"Oh, god," he said. "Well, don't worry, we'll get you a good wagon of your own. We'll take care of you."

Chapter Sixteen

What with all the movement and the uneasy moments of that morning, by the time a horse and wagon was acquired for us my head was bleeding again. I was not supposed to be so active, Dr. Powers had told me back at Leavenworth. But I had not paid mind to what he had said.

Of course, our Yankee soldier now had to see to my bleeding head. It would not look good to see this caravan rolling along with people sitting in the wagons and bleeding, would it?

He said something about stopping to visit the doctor

who had his own traveling surgery up ahead. I tried to tell him I did not need a doctor, just a new bandage.

"Only place you'll get that is in the doctor's surgery," he told me. "So let's go."

"Well, then, I want Martha with me."

"You're a sassy little piece." He sounded a lot like Seth, so I forgave him and went along, leaving Martha to the reins of the horse and our place in the caravan.

I do believe that the doctor was in his cups. I had never really seen Seth in his cups, but of course it is general knowledge in these parts that the measure of a man can be taken by the way he holds his liquor. They say Seth can hold his like a first-rate gentleman. This doctor could not. But what can you expect from anybody from the North?

That is to say, he was not totally drunk. He could function as a physician, I will not dispute that, but still his hands shook and his words were somewhat slurred as he unwound the bandage from my head.

"Damned nasty business, the collapse of that building," he told me, as if I didn't already know. "And as for Quantrill's response, the burning of Lawrence, why the *New York Daily Times* called all of them 'fiends incarnate.'"

Then, "You're going to have a scar on your forehead the rest of your life, girl. Do you still get dizzy?"

"I get the mumblefuddles," I told him.

He sighed. "That's good enough for me." He re-wrapped my head, gave me some clean bandages, then some powders to take, and sent me on my way.

I suppose the mumblefuddles are the same in the North as well as the South. *We speak a common language,* I thought. *It's really unfair to be killing each other.*

MARTHA AND I traveled for two days in our new wagon. The horse, named Precious, was middling passable. The roads were rutted. Sometimes the dust from all those wagon wheels choked us. Sometimes what choked us was the smoky haze that hung in the air from the landscape that still burned as we went along. At night, when the caravan stopped, it got almost cold and we huddled together in our cloaks. September days were still hot. Skies were still a hard blue and the landscape all around us was aglow with colorful wildflowers, but I saw none of it.

I only knew that I wanted to go home, to stop playing this childish game now, to call it quits. I would have given an arm to see Seth come casually riding over the horizon, and on pulling up to where I was sleeping say,

"Hey, Juliet, you up? Come on, I've got something to show you."

I cried at night. I couldn't help it. I was mindful of Martha trying to shush me, of her enfolding me in her arms, of the terrible cuts and sores inside my soul. Finally on the second night, I asked her, "Martha, where are we going? Where are we going to go?"

She had no answer for me except "Something will come up, Juliet. Something will happen to save us. Have faith."

On that second night as I went back to sleep, tears staining my face, something did happen.

We were kidnapped.

Chapter Seventeen

I WAS SLEEPING fitfully when a hand came over my mouth and I heard a man's voice in my ear. "Don't be afraid. Don't scream. We're going to take you away from here."

Next to me I heard Martha struggling. Then Seth's voice. "It's all right, girls. We've come to take you away."

Martha becalmed herself. So did I. Next thing you know, I was lifted in somebody's strong arms, but not Seth's. It was a moonless night. "My pillowcase," I whispered, "it has all my things."

I was allowed to retrieve it, and I suppose Seth let

Martha have hers. Then we were whisked away into the nearby woods, soundlessly. There was a stream. They waded through it. I assumed that the man carrying me was a guerrilla. I could feel the stitching on his shirt. A few more yards and I heard horses nickering. I could smell them, and the leather saddles. Then I was lifted and put onto the back of one and my rescuer mounted and picked up the reins and quieted his mount. "Easy, girl."

"Hello, Juliet, how you doin'?"

"Seth!" I managed a sob.

"Hush, no crying here, girl. Let's go, Bill."

So it was Bill Anderson, Martha's older brother. How lucky she was to have her brother and her husband come tearing through the night like heroes in a fairy tale to rescue her.

I clung to Bill's waist and he had his horse follow Seth's. Not on the road but through fields and woods on trails only they knew about. Talk was intermittent. They asked how we felt. Had we been treated well? There were no words on that subject. How can you tell about witnessing the death and burial of a three-year-old boy?

Our silence was taken as testimony by Seth, and he let go with a handsome round of curses, then fell silent.

"I'll kill them all," Bill said. It was the way he said it that sent chills through me, like someone would say "It's raining outside," or "I'll take the gravy now, please."

"Martha is sickly," I told Seth.

"You're not so robust yourself," she answered back. Then to Seth, "She had to go to the Yankee doctor the other day. Her head was bleeding. She's supposed to rest and doesn't."

"We'll get you to a place to rest," Seth promised.

"Where?" I asked.

"My place," he said. "We're going back to my place."

It was a two-day ride back to Seth's place, or at least a ride that required an overnight camp in the fields or woods. We stopped at sundown, only because Seth was afraid for my health. And Martha's.

They had food with them, beef jerky and other trail food, coffee to brew, and some canned sardines they'd taken off dead federal soldiers. At supper they talked of the war and of the other girls still at Leavenworth too maimed to travel.

Jenny Anderson was dead, of course, but now we found out that Mary survived but was crippled in the head. Fanny was still recuperating in the hospital. Bill Anderson's face went dark when he spoke of it. "So many dead," he said. "I have a personal vendetta to fight now. To hell with the Yankees."

Then Seth took me aside and undid the bandage on my head, washed the wound, bandaged it again tightly, and gave me some of the medicine Dr. Powers had sent along.

"You're not as angry as Bill is," I told him.

"Some people have to let it out. Do things," he said. "You should know. He isn't the same as before the building fell and he lost Jenny. He thinks nothing of killing Yankees now. People are starting to call him 'Bloody Bill.'"

I gave a snort. "Not Bill."

He nodded silently. "He always did have a streak of violence in him. But he managed to keep it under cover. No more. You see that silk ribbon he's got tied to his horse's bridle with the knots in it?"

"Yes."

"It's from the sash of Jenny's dress. He puts a new knot in it for every man he kills."

I felt dizzy. "Oh. But why do you tell me this?"

"It's always best to be informed," he said. "Know the person you're talking to. So be careful with him, will you?"

I hugged him. It was a long, meaningful hug on both our parts, erasing every argument we'd ever had, sealing agreements we'd not yet made. "What would I do without you, Seth? Oh, I missed you so much!"

Chapter Eighteen

As if that wasn't enough to bring tears to my eyes, a bit later, before bed, Bill Anderson suggested that he and I "move away from the newlyweds a bit and give them some privacy."

So we did. We moved quite a bit apart from them, near the creek, and Bill built another fire and soon I was asleep beside it.

In the middle of the night I awoke, feeling someone standing over me.

It was Bill.

"What is it?" I asked.

"It's starting to rain. The creek may rise. We'd better move."

"What are Seth and Martha doing?"

"Can't see 'em from here. But I'll wager he's left the place already. And he trusts me to get you out of here."

I felt an uneasiness about the whole thing. I sat up. "Let's go make sure they've left."

He put a restraining hand on my shoulder. "You wouldn't want to walk in on the bride and groom at an inappropriate moment, would you? Come on. Rain's getting heavier. There's a bit of a cave farther on in the woods. I know Seth knows it's there. C'mon, get your things."

I obeyed. After all, he was the head of Martha's family. And Seth had warned me to be careful with him, whatever that meant. So I gathered up my pillowcase, my blanket, put on my boots, and let him lead me and the horse across some rocky ground toward the woods.

A bit away from the camp we'd made he lighted a pine-knot torch so he could see better and it came to me then: He was prepared for this. This was no sudden act of God, rain or no rain. And when we did reach the woods there was no cave. Only us and the horse, and by then I was growing positively brilliant.

He was taking me away from Seth.

But what for? My mind whirled. My thoughts tumbled with possibilities. Seth had said nothing about this. Why had he let me go when Bill suggested we move out of his and Martha's presence back at their camp? What was going on?

I decided to display the one characteristic that Seth disliked in me. Boldness. "Nobody likes a bold young girl," he always said.

I quickened my pace to catch up with Bill. "You're taking me away from my brother and Martha," I said, "aren't you?"

"Now be a good girl and don't make a fuss. For just a little while, yes."

"But why?"

"You won't understand."

"After what I've been through these last few weeks, you'd be surprised at what I'd understand," I said firmly. "I'm not a little girl anymore."

"You'll always be a little girl to me, Juliet. Just like Jenny. You are just like her." He paused, and in the flickering light of the torch he peered at me. "I'm taking you away for a while, yes. Because you look so much like Jenny. And I miss her like purple hell. And I want to be with you alone for a little bit and just look at you and talk with you and hear you laugh and push back your hair and do all the things big brothers do. Because those are all the things that Seth does. And why the hell should he have you and Martha, too? You have Jenny's arms and Jenny's hands and Jenny's mouth. Oh, you don't know what it does to me, watching you."

My heart was beating very fast, hearing all this.

This man is a lunatic, I told myself. Seth said he wasn't the same as he was before the building fell. Well, Seth doesn't know the half of it.

"I'd like to teach you things," he said. "Things I wanted to teach Jenny but didn't have the time. Will you let me?"

Fear was both a hot and a cold river running through my veins. "If you don't let me go back to Seth, I'll scream."

He hit me then. Not on the face, thank goodness, because my head was hurting again. He grabbed my wrist and whirled me around and gave my bottom a wallop. I cried out.

"You want a gag?" he asked. "I can give you one."

I said no. "But where's the cave?"

He laughed. "There isn't any. Just had to get on with you. Get us going."

"Where?"

"Where? Well, truth to tell, Juliet, I'm on my way to Texas."

I stopped. "You really are kidnapping me. Why? I never did anything bad to you, Bill Anderson. Are you going to kill me? I know they call you Bloody Bill. I know what those knots in the ribbon on your horse are for. And now you want to put one on there for me, don't you?"

He smiled. "By my sainted mother, you've got the same sand in you that Jenny had. No, I don't want to kill you. I told you, I just want to spend time with you, get to know you. I suspect it'll help clear my mind about Jenny. Now can't you do that little favor for an old fool like me?"

One minute showing violence and the next making a person pity him. "Yes," I said, "specially since Seth told me to be careful of you."

He stopped and pulled a whiskey flask out of his back pocket, took a couple of swigs, and offered it to me.

"No, thank you, I don't drink," I declined politely.

"That brother of yours never let you have a taste, did he? Just like he never let you shoot a gun. Well, before this little trip is over we'll remedy both those problems."

"Bill, please let me go back to Seth. Please."

He smiled. "Love him, do you?"

"He's the only family I've got left. He looks after me."

"I'll look after you these next few days. I told you that. Now hush."

I hushed. My head was pounding as I struggled to keep up. Finally I felt my head bleeding again, put my hand up there, and it came away with blood on it. Now I was angry. And I stopped walking. He was about thirty feet away from me when he realized I wasn't with him anymore.

He turned and held out the pine-knot torch. "Where are you?"

"I can't walk anymore."

"What are you, a Sissy Mary, that you have to stop?"

"No. My head's bleeding again. And I'm dizzy."

He came back to me, saw the blood, and cussed. "Damn, why do I have to get a damaged one?" he asked himself.

"This was your idea, not mine."

"You mind your tongue, girl. I take no sass from any of my sisters and I'll take none from you. What have you got for your head?"

I reached inside the pillowcase and got out the bandages and the laudanum the doctor had said to sprinkle on the wound. He fixed it for me with surprisingly gentle hands. Then he looked at the sky, decided it would soon be first light, and told me we'd be best off traveling nights and sleeping days.

We'd miss Seth and Martha if they came looking for us. But this was how he wanted it.

Back again in the woods, he made a clearing and another small fire. This time he shot a rabbit and insisted on showing me how to skin it. I'd never had to do this before. Never had Pa or Maxine or Seth made me. In our house, before the Yankees came, food was always plentiful, and if it was duck or rabbit, the first time I met it was on a good china plate, all done up with mashed potatoes and spinach and gravy, with candlelight and polite conversation at home.

That you had to shoot it or otherwise kill it first, I knew. But I was never made to watch, much less partake in the killing or skinning.

I cried when he showed me. I threw up. He laughed and told me that was exactly how Jenny had acted, but before she died she could do it like an old-time hunter.

"Next you learn to kill it," he promised.

I could scarce eat it. *Oh Seth,* I wondered, chewing it like it was taffy. *Where are you?*

Chapter Nineteen

"QUANTRILL WANTS to establish a winter camp in Texas," Bill Anderson was telling me. "That's what I'm supposed to be doing now. Heading to cross the Red River into Grayson County. We have some people there already. They sent a courier to tell Quantrill that the river is a hellhole, full of quicksand bogs, and to take the ferry. And that they found a good spot for the camp on Mineral Creek. But Quantrill wants me to put my stamp on it before he heads down there. Doesn't trust the scouts. Trusts me. Whadd'ya think of that?"

He was sitting next to the fire, smoking a cheroot. I

was scrubbing out the coffeepot with sand after nearly throwing up my supper of rabbit that I'd helped skin. He'd made me take a dose of the horrible whiskey to settle my stomach. I almost died from the taste of it, the way it burned going down, but then a peculiar thing happened: I got all warm inside and I didn't want to throw up anymore.

Girls do the dishes after supper, Bill had told me. At least his sisters always did, always helped the help. And a campout was no different from a fancy dining room. I didn't argue, afraid of what he might do to me.

"The courier said there's plenty of forage for the horses in Texas, and the creek is full of turtles and the like, catfish and trout. The woods are full of pigs and deer. I'd like to get there sooner than soon and make my own report to Quantrill. Do you understand?"

I nodded yes. "But I may be holding you back."

"No, ma'am," he answered. "You keep me company and that'll get me there faster. Two heads are better than one. And you lookin' so much like Jenny, well, it keeps me cheerful. I like teaching you things. We're out here in the hinterland enough so we can travel days now. And tomorrow I'm gonna teach you to shoot."

I lay there under the stars unable to sleep. I could easily slip away, I knew, if not for the fact that I did not know where I was, so there was no sense in escaping.

But lying awake was a good thing, too. For in the night lit only by a crescent moon, I saw forms moving in the nearby woods, and I trembled with fear.

Someone is out there, spying on us. No. Several someones.

I could do nothing. I felt helpless with Bloody Bill Anderson sleeping on the other side of the fire. If I woke him, what would he do? How far did the name "Bloody Bill" go with him? Would he kill them all? And if I didn't alert him, would they kill us?

Wait. Suppose the creeping dark forms were Seth and Martha and some friends come to get me?

I wanted to throw up again. I decided I needed more whiskey, so I crawled around the fire, as quietly as I could, to where Bill's flask lay beside him.

Luckily, my fate was decided for me. I knocked it over.

Before I knew what hit me, two hands grasped my wrists in an ironlike grip. "What are you doing, miss?"

"I need some whiskey."

"You? You *need*? What you need is a good spanking, I'm thinking."

"No. You don't understand. I'm going to throw up."

"Why?"

I bit my lower lip. I pointed to the woods. "There're people out there. Creeping around."

At once he was crouched down next to me, checking the revolvers at his waist, picking up his rifle, putting on his hat. "Get down and stay down," he ordered.

I did so. But I started to cry, too. "I want my brother, Seth." I did my crying quietly.

"You shut up about Seth. I'm your brother from here on. Get used to it."

For some reason, while he was scolding me in harsh whispers, our pursuers had gone out of sight. "Now see what you've done?" he mumbled, as if I were personally responsible for picking them up and putting them down someplace else. "How the hell do I know where they are now?"

"We're right here, mister," a voice behind us said. "So don't you take no notion of shooting. Matter of fact, why don't you put those guns of yourn on the ground?"

And he poked a stick into Bill's back. Likely feeling that he was cornered by a fox, Bill set down his rifle, then his four Navy Colt revolvers, and we turned around to face three of the most disreputable characters on the face of the earth.

One picked up Bill's rifle. "What do they call you?" he asked.

Bill didn't answer, and even I didn't want him shot at that juncture, because Seth always said, "Don't trade off the devil you've got for one you don't know."

"Anderson," I told them. "His name is Bill Anderson. Bloody Bill Anderson."

"And you?" the man asked. "You his child bride? Or what?"

"She's my sister," Bill said.

"Then why she look so scared?"

"'Cause she don't wanna go to Texas with me. But she's goin'."

"Bloody Bill," the man repeated. "You wouldn't be with Quantrill's Raiders, would you?"

"Yes, he would," I answered. "And if you harm us, Quantrill will kill you."

"And now that the pleasantries are over," Bill said, "who the hell are you all?"

The man relaxed a bit. In spite of his torn clothing, unshaven face, and the shoeless feet of his two younger companions, and their accumulated dirt and lack of firearms, he bore himself like an officer in the Confederate army. "We're part of the many affected by Order

Number 11. We've no place to go. We missed the wagon train and are just wandering the earth like the Lord's people in the Bible. And there are hundreds of others like us out here." He gestured with his head to the woods.

For a moment there was silence, and a wolf howled in the distance. Then our visitor came over and took all of Bill's weapons. After which he made us remove our shoes and hand them over.

"Sister, is it?" he said to me. "Well, I for one don't believe it. And as we proceed on, we'll tell everybody we met you. What's your name, little sweetie?"

"Juliet Bradshaw."

He handed the revolvers over to his companions and tossed the rifle aside, out into the darkness. "You find that tomorrow. By then we'll be long since gone," he told Bill.

I was surprised that they didn't take Bill's horse and all our supplies. But they didn't. They just took our shoes and walked off, polite as you please, to the east, where the sky was already getting lighter and the sun promised us a kiss if we'd wait up for her another hour or two.

Bill was cussing. "Damned nice of them to leave me a rifle," he said. "Lie down, Juliet, and go to sleep. And don't give me no sass."

Chapter Twenty

"WISH THOSE damn fools had left me my Colt revolver instead of this rifle," Bill was grumbling. "I'd rather teach you to shoot with a revolver any day. First off, you can't ride and shoot a rifle at the same time. You can't load the rifle while you're riding. And with a Navy Colt, why, you can carry four of them at a time and keep shooting. Well, anyway, you know this is a Sharpe's carbine and the Union rifles are only muzzle-loading, single shot."

I didn't know, but I said yes.

"Well, come on over here, and I'll show you how to hold it. Get you used to it."

Reluctantly, I went over to him. "Seth isn't going to like my doing this," I said.

"You don't shoot, you get no breakfast."

I was about starved. The smell of the bacon in the fry pan over the morning fire made my stomach growl. Same for the bubbling coffee. We were going to have a shooting lesson first, however, he'd told me. And if I didn't shoot, I didn't eat all day.

I had to get away from this man, I determined, as I walked over to him. He was crazier than a hooty owl. I stood next to him, and he positioned the Sharpe's rifle in my arms and aimed it at a rock in the distance, toward the east.

It was then that we saw the rider. On the horizon. Like a silhouette cut out of black paper against the red sky.

"Who in purple hell is that?" he asked.

I blinked to adjust my eyes to the sunrise and said I didn't know.

"It's a woman," he said disgustedly. "I can see her billowing skirts. You leave any women friends back there in the wagon train?"

"No. Bill, the gun is hurting my shoulder."

He adjusted it and went on with the shooting lesson. He showed me how to take aim, to hold the gun steady, to hold myself steady, to plant my feet in the ground so the recoil from the shot wouldn't knock me back and down. I reminded him that I had no shoes, that they'd been stolen, and that the ground was full of stones. I couldn't very well plant my feet, could I? At least he had an extra pair of boots for himself.

"No sass," he said. "Just do as I say."

Somehow I dug my feet in and managed to pull the trigger. The recoil almost did knock me down, would have, too, if Bill wasn't standing behind me. "Good," he said, "that was good. Next time you'll be less afraid. We'll do more later this afternoon."

The woman on the horse still sat there, not moving, though the shot had echoed through the quiet morning with a sound that was almost blasphemous.

We went to have our breakfast. Bill cracked open some eggs into the fry pan with the bacon. "This afternoon, we come to a creek," he said, "you're gonna get out of those clothes of yours and bathe and put on something clean. You got another dress?"

"Just one more. But I can't wear it."

"Why?"

"It was"—I breathed softly—"Jenny's."

He did not look at me. "You're still gonna get cleaned up."

Something was wrong here. "Just in case you're getting notions, I'm not going to get out of my clothes in front of you," I told him firmly.

He shoved bacon and eggs into his mouth. "Hell's bells, girl. I've seen all my sisters in all states of undress. Never thought a thing of it. Neither did they."

"Well, in my house there was only me and Seth. And we respected each other's privacy. And I don't believe that Martha never thought a thing of it."

He laughed. "All that's over with now. It was part of civilization, families living together in houses and respecting each other's privacy and such. The world got shed of that the minute the fool war started."

"I recollect my pa saying something about that before the Yankees came 'round," I told him.

"Oh? What did he say?"

"He said we had to hold fast to the things that made us civilized now that war was here. He said that no matter what happened, we must remember the small everyday things that made up civilization or we were whipped before we started."

He gazed at the horizon where the woman still sat her horse. "Well, he's dead, your pa. Most of his stripe are by now. We killed lots of 'em in Lawrence."

"I'm still not taking my clothes off in front of you," I said.

"We'll see," he returned.

I began to tremble and wonder how he had come to be, the Bill Anderson who now sat in front of me shoveling his food into his mouth. He was certainly not the Bill Anderson I had grown up knowing, the Bill Anderson his sisters had worshipped so. All the times our paths had crossed he'd been polite and gentlemanly, a good friend to Seth, caring of his own sisters. *He's changed,* Seth had warned me. *Since that building collapsed. They call him Bloody Bill now.*

Could one person change that much?

I looked at the horizon and the woman on the horse. And in my bones I knew one true thing.

She was there for me. To watch me. And when we moved she would follow at a discreet distance. And if the time came when we happened upon a creek and Bill made me take off my clothes, all I had to do was put up a fight and she'd come galloping over to help me. All she was waiting for was to catch Bill treating me badly. Then she'd pounce. Who she was I did not know.

Maybe she was dead Jenny come to save me from her brother.

The Andersons were good Catholics. Jenny would say she was the Blessed Mother come to save me. I didn't care if it was the wife of the devil himself as long as she was on my side.

I got up and scraped off my dish and poured Bill a second cup of coffee, which I knew by now he liked. I reached for my pillowcase to get another pair of stockings to put on my feet, and Charity McCorkle Kerr's doll fell out on the ground. I reached for it, but Bill had it in his grasp first.

"What's this? You still play with dolls?"

"No. It belonged to Charity McCorkle Kerr. She's dead now."

"I know damned well she's dead. You ought to give it to her husband. Or her brother. Either one."

He took it and put it in his saddlebag. "I'll give it to her brother," he promised. "It'll mean more to him. What's wrong? You don't like the idea? You'd rather I throw it up in the air and show you how this Sharpe's rifle can blow it to bits before it starts to come down?"

"No, give it to her brother," I said. "Do." No sense in provoking him now. I put on my stockings and to my surprise he told me to mount his horse or we'd never make any time that day. He'd walk beside me. I thanked him.

"No need for thanks. I just want to get out of sight of that siren on the horizon," he said. "And find the nearest creek, fast as we can."

I was given orders not to look back at the "siren" as we left our camp. So I didn't dare.

And then, before we'd gone a mile I knew who it was. And quiet tears came down my face.

Chapter Twenty-one

WE RODE mostly through desert that day and soon realized what a trap we were in. As the hours passed and the sun beat down, we could find no shelter at all, much less a creek. I didn't have a hat, and the burden of the sun got worse on my head, making it impossible for me to breathe, provoking my wound, and burning my face and shoulders.

Bill Anderson felt it, too, I could tell. But he said nothing, just kept walking, like a man who had found the dark side of his moon and was comfortable with it.

Insects droned, tumbleweeds blew in the hot wind, snakes slithered, and Bill said we were in a valley. It was very stony in some places; in others, a very coarse, gritty sand covered the ground.

"We should be coming on to some falls soon," he said.

Falls meant water.

"Get down off the horse," he directed.

I did so. When my feet hit the ground, I was surprised at the heat of it. And my head was beginning to spin again. But I stood very still.

Bill pulled me aside and slapped the rump of his horse and it took off like it was running a race.

"What are you doing?" I demanded.

"He'll find the water faster than we can. He likely smells it already. We've only to follow his footsteps in the sand."

While I had the opportunity, I looked behind us to where the lady rider should be.

She was still there, a good distance behind us to be sure, but close enough to keep an eye on us. And, I noticed, she wore a hat.

I felt my own discomfort mounting. Now not only my head throbbed but my face was burned, as were my shoulders and arms, and my stomach was churning.

"I can't go any farther," I told Bill. "I hurt all over."

"Nonsense," he said. "This isn't Seth Bradshaw's sister talking, is it? I thought you had more spirit than that. Anyway, what are you fixing on doing? Sitting here in this desert under the noonday sun?"

"You shouldn't have taken us here under the noonday sun."

"Well, I thought there would be more cover. Rocks. And caves. All right, Miss Perfect? God, I'm glad you're not my sister."

"So am I."

While this debate was going on, we were following in the horse's footsteps. And sure enough, I heard the roaring sound of a waterfall up ahead. There, filling himself to his heart's content, was the horse, drinking from a small pond into which the falls emptied. It was like a scene from heaven.

I forgot all about the danger the water could bring to me and ran to it, reached it before Bill Anderson did, took off my stockings, sat on a rock, and put my sore and burning feet into the coolness of the water.

Bill stripped off his shirt and threw it aside. Then he started removing his boots and trousers. I turned away and got myself out of that vicinity quick and found myself another place that was blessedly shielded by a rock. If any bathing was to be done on my part, I would do it right here.

I was just going to fetch my pillowcase where my lavender soap was when Bill Anderson came upon me, dripping wet. Thank heaven he was in his smallclothes from the waist down.

"Remember, you promised to bathe, proper-like. What are you waiting for?"

"I promised nothing." Oh how I longed to dive into the pond, to float around in there, to take off my bandage and put my whole head under and let the blessed water do its own healing.

He reached out his hand. "Come on. No time better than the present to cast off all those childish scruples."

I moved from him. Fast. I ran to the far side of the pond where there were three ledges of black marble over which the water tumbled. He near had me once and I screamed and stopped to pick up a freshwater shell on the ground and threw it at him.

It hit him on the forehead and there was blood.

"You little witch," he said. "Now I'll show you who's boss." He ran over to where his trousers were, grabbed his belt, and started swinging it at me.

I screamed some more. They were ragged, frightened prayers to heaven, and they did not go unanswered. Out of the corner of my eye I saw a cloud of dust and heard horse's hooves, and of a sudden there she was in the middle of it all, Colt revolver drawn and aimed at Bill.

"Back off, you damned bully. Away from that girl."

I recognized the voice, oh I did. I stopped, breathing heavily. My head was drumming, my feet hurt, and I was sobbing. Bill Anderson couldn't have looked more surprised if it had been the Blessed Mother sitting that horse with pistols drawn.

"You earned the name Bloody Bill honestly," the woman said, "and everybody respects you for it. Well, when I tell them about this they'll no longer respect you. Tormenting a little girl who's been through six kinds of hell already."

"Sue Mundy, what in purple hell are you doing here?" Bill Anderson asked.

"Chasing you. And it's a good thing I caught you first, before her big brother did, or you'd be lying dead, a fossil before your time. But not before he beat the daylights out of you."

"Is my brother here?" I asked in disbelief.

"No, child. He discovered you were missing, and he

and I decided to take different routes to try to find you. He had to make arrangements to send Martha back to his ranch in the holler first, though. She couldn't make the trip. I came west. He went north. Only reason I found you was because I came across some refugees who told me about running across you and whereabouts you were." While she was talking, she was tying Bill's hands behind his back. With his own belt.

"I saw you from a distance, watching us. At first I didn't know who you were."

"I thought you were on our side," Bill Anderson said.

"What side is that? The side that tortures little girls? And tries to get them to take off their clothes? Enough talk now. You go on around that rock and take your bath, child. We'll stay here. Nobody will bother you. I promise."

"There're catfish in the pond," I told her. "They make good eating."

"Good idea. We'll eat, then I'll bring Bloody Bill back to Seth Bradshaw. See what he wants to do with him."

"I'm supposed to be on my way to Texas for Quantrill," Bill said in a pleading voice.

"Oh, you'll go to Texas all right," Sue Mundy said. "After Seth Bradshaw gets done with you."

SUE MUNDY and my brother had a plan. They were to meet the next day at a place called Sulphur Springs, one mile from Seth's ranch, whether or not either of them found me. They were to regroup and, if I was not yet found, they would recruit some other Quantrill Raiders and organize a real search party, rather than just wander aimlessly around the desert.

I had so many questions my head was spinning, as if it wasn't spinning enough from the pain of my fall.

Did Seth know yet that Sue Mundy was a man? The last I recollected, he wouldn't discuss it at Fort Leavenworth hospital and I was determined to let the whole matter die there.

I supposed Seth didn't. Marcellus Jerome Clark still had a lot of work to do as Sue Mundy and wasn't about to bandy any secrets around to give away his identity.

Before we left on the trip to Sulphur Springs, Sue Mundy bandaged my head good again and even combed out my hair. "A woman doesn't feel human unless her hair is decent looking," she said.

How did Marcellus Jerome Clark know such things?

Chapter Twenty-two

I HADN'T SEEN Seth since the night he and Bill had crept into our camp when we were with the wagon train to nowhere and they rushed us out of there.

Now here he was at Sulphur Springs, a mile from his home, waiting alone with his horse before a small fire and smoking a cheroot.

He got up when we approached, his hand going instinctively to his revolver at his hip. His face broke into a grin, and he came over to help me off the horse.

"God, you look like hell. Where you been? To the briar patch?"

I just put my arms around him, hugging him tight

and sobbing against his middle. I didn't want to let go, and he held me close, kissing the top of my head.

"Hey, c'mon, what happened?" Then he spoke in low tones, saying hello to Bill Anderson, then seeing his hands tied.

"Why is he tied up?" he asked Sue Mundy.

"He was taking her to Texas."

"Why?"

"Ask him, why don't you."

So Seth did. "You kidnapped my sister? You gone 'round the bend, Bill? Why?"

"She looks so much like Jenny," came the soft reply.

"Then," asked Seth, "why didn't you treat her better? What *did* you do to her, anyway?" Then Seth cursed and picked me up, and I went all limp in his arms. I heard him tell Sue Mundy to tie Bill to a tree; he wanted to talk to me first and find out the truth of the matter.

We sat a small distance from the fire. Crazily, I concentrated on the sparks it sent up into the night. Crazily, I wondered if Sue Mundy had told Seth yet that she was really a man.

"Did he hurt you in any way?" Seth questioned softly.

His eyes bore into me. I said no. He'd just swung his belt at me because I wouldn't do as he wanted.

"What did he want?" Seth asked carefully.

There was no lying to Seth. He could smell lies five miles away. "For me to take my clothes off and go into the pond of water and wash," I said.

I saw something come into his face, something hard and fierce. "And? I have to know, Juliet. If he dishonored you at all, I have to call him out."

"You mean duel?"

"Yes. It's still the order of the day, amongst men who care about their women. So tell me."

"Course not, Seth. He had it fixed in his head that I should, that there's a war on and that means there're no more rules of civilization."

"Said that, did he?"

"Yes."

He reached out and touched the side of my face, gently. "And that's when Sue Mundy came to your rescue?"

"Yes, but I knew she was there. We both saw her for a whole day before, though he didn't know who she was. I knew I couldn't fight off Bill myself. I kind of knew that at the right time Sue would come and save me. But just the same, I picked up a big shell and threw it at him. Hit him in the head, too. Made him bleed."

"You're a good girl, Juliet. I'm proud of you. Did he hurt you in any other way?"

I fell silent and looked at the fire.

"You can tell me," he pushed. "You can tell me anything. I have to know, child."

I faced him square, then. There were tears in the corners of my eyes. "All right, you want to know, I'll tell you. He hit me once because I said I would scream. He made me drink whiskey. Taught me how. And you know what, Seth? I was throwing up because of the wild rabbit he made me eat, and the whiskey settled my innards."

"What else?"

"Made me skin the rabbit."

"The dirty low-down son of a skunk. I'll kill him."

"You can't kill him. Not on my account. Or you'll be as bad as he is then."

"I can't kill him because I'm married to his sister. Don't you think I know that? But I can beat him up enough to make him wish he were dead." He got up and helped me to my feet. We walked back to where Sue Mundy was frying some bacon. It was all she had in the way of food, but it smelled so good my stomach hurt. Seth's house was but a mile away but none of us wanted to drag Martha into this now.

"Sue will see to you," he told me. "Do as she says. I do believe she's got some nice warm clothes in that saddlebag of hers."

Sue Mundy and I exchanged looks. Hers said, don't worry, it'll be all right. Mine said, you saved my life twice, I trust you.

Seth took out his revolver and untied Bloody Bill, then Seth took him off to the woods, which were all charred and blackened because of the fires the Yankees had lighted. They went down a hill, and I said a prayer that Seth wouldn't kill him. Sue found me some warm clothes because it was more chilly here than in the desert, and then I had supper of bacon and bread and coffee.

Chapter Twenty-three

IT CAME to me from other sources, I don't recollect how—on the night wind, I suppose—that Seth Bradshaw beat the purple demons out of Bill Anderson, although Bill Anderson did his share of destruction to Seth, too.

What made it all worse was that Seth and Bill had been friends since childhood. They had sown their wild oats together. They had drunk themselves into oblivion together. They had taken part in horse races, in playing cards, even courted the same girls.

Neither had a brother. What more could be said? When they came back to camp that night, I was supposed to be sleeping in the tent Sue Mundy put me in. Half groggy from the laudanum she'd given me, I listened behind its canvas wall.

It took me no time at all to perceive that Seth was, at that very minute, sending Bill off to Texas. "And if you come back to these parts too soon, consider me the enemy. Just as much as if I wore blue."

He supplied him with beef jerky, water, his horse, and one blanket. Also his Sharpe's rifle.

I knew my brother well enough to understand that you never wanted to be considered his enemy. It was worse than being shot with a Sharpe's rifle. I felt bad. And I didn't know how to act with Seth now. Did he blame any of this on me? And when word got to Martha, as I knew it would, how would she regard me? Would she say I'd teased Bill? That was the ultimate sin a young girl could commit hereabouts. To be a tease to a nice, decent boy like Bill Anderson.

I had to let both of them know I wasn't. And, I decided, I had to let Seth know tonight.

That was one problem I had facing me. The other was simple enough: I had to keep Sue Mundy from sleeping in the tent with me.

I didn't want Marcellus Jerome Clark cuddling me. So how would I manage this?

I decided that the lies we all had between us were going to kill us before the Yankees did, and so I got up, wrapped a blanket around myself, and went out into the starlit night as if to my own execution. I might, I decided, have to tell Seth the truth about Sue Mundy, again, to save my decency.

My moon was growing darker.

"What are you doing up? You're supposed to be sleeping."

"Seth, I have to talk to you."

He gave me a look. He was seated by the fire, holding a wet cloth just below his left eye. When he took the cloth away I could see the bruise, already turning purple. There was also a cut on his bottom lip and on his forehead. "Something you forgot to tell me before?"

"No." I knew him well enough not to mention his wounds. "But something I should tell you now."

"Go on."

"I just want you to know that I didn't tease Bill Anderson. I never sashayed around him like a cheap saloon girl."

"What do you know about cheap saloon girls?"

"Seth, you know what I mean. I just didn't want you thinking that."

"I don't. I know you better. You couldn't sashay if your life depended on it."

"I'll have to tell Martha that, too."

"Go easy with Martha. I don't know how I'm going to tell her about her brother and what happened yet. Is there anything else?" He threw a log on the fire.

"Yes. I don't want Sue Mundy in the tent with me tonight." I looked around for her. "Where is she?"

"Washing out some clothes at the end of the springs. God, that water has got a sulphur smell to it. So why don't you want her?"

"Seth, don't scold now. Or get mad. Promise?"

"Honey, I'm so glad to have you back in one piece, I couldn't get mad at you tonight for anything."

The words warmed me. I sat down next to him, gathered my blanket around me, and leaned on his arm. "I can't have her in the tent with me because she's a man, Seth. She told me she was."

"I know."

"You *know*?"

"Yes. I've been around her enough to figure that out.

Your old brother isn't that dense when it comes to women."

"Did you tell her you know?"

"Course not. Her work all depends on her keeping it a secret. How you got it out of her, I'll never know."

"She wanted me to tell you. Because you were smitten with her. And she didn't want that. And that's why she, or he, kissed me. To prove she was telling the truth."

He gave a deep sigh. "I'm not so certain that was the whole reason. You sure there isn't anybody I can marry you off to, at twelve?"

"I'll be thirteen soon."

"God help me."

"Seth, she told me on the way here that nobody must know she's a man. She said she has no currency with the Yankees as a man. That they'd kill her. But that they like her as a woman. If we give her away, Seth, she's dead."

"But she fights with us as Lieutenant Flowers. I suppose that's all part of the act, and as long as the Yankees know it's an act, they are intrigued by her. Just think, Juliet, someday we'll be able to say we knew her."

I hugged him wordlessly.

He kissed my forehead. "You're a dear little thing for keeping her—his—secret. There's something about you,

Juliet, everybody confides in you. I think it's your eyes. They're so sad."

"It's 'cause I got you for a brother," I teased. "Always bossing me around."

He smiled. "Go to bed," he said.

Chapter Twenty-four

A T FIRST there was some discussion about Seth coming back to his place with us at all. Since the destruction of Lawrence, Kansas, the 450 men in Quantrill's band had been on the run, setting up camps in different places. They were pursued by home-guard units, civilian posses, cavalry troops, and militia who were out to kill them.

These Yankee searchers combed woods, fields, houses, and barns. They came upon men at their supper tables and shot them dead. They, who criticized the method of killing employed by Quantrill's men in Lawrence, hanged men working in their barnyards, whether they had taken part in the Lawrence killings or not.

By the end of August they had killed at least eighty men. They took no prisoners. Now, in September, the military had run out of ammunition, their horses were worn down, and the officers were discouraged and disorganized.

But still, a meeting between a Yankee and any member of Quantrill's band meant certain death for one or the other.

Seth wanted to seek out and rejoin Quantrill, who had established a new camp on the Stanley farm, which was soon discovered by the federals. So he moved to a new site on the east fork of the Little Blue River, only to be discovered again. All the time he was out searching for me, Seth kept getting intelligence, via a messenger, as to where Quantrill was. After all, Seth was important to Quantrill. He was a captain.

Next, Quantrill bivouacked at Joe Dillingham's farm, a good hideout because it had only one route in. Still, just about the time we set off for Seth's farm, Quantrill passed the word along that his men should meet on September 30 at Captain Perdee's farm on the Blackwater River in Johnson County.

Having received that intelligence, Seth decided to go with us to his place. After all, he did yearn to see Martha. And it was only September 12. There was time yet to meet up with Quantrill.

The first thing Seth did was change his clothes for the trip home. Off came the gray Quantrill shirt with the red stitching. The baggy trousers, another sign of Quantrill's men, got pulled out of the high cavalry boots and the four revolvers worn around the hips were reduced to two.

He had Sue Mundy cut his hair, after which she started off to join Quantrill. Most of the Raiders had longer hair and Seth had his cut to look more conventional. He had started growing sideburns and so he shaved them off. The hat with the round brim went and was replaced with a Confederate soldier's cap, which he'd kept in his saddlebags.

Now he was ready.

We rode through what was already being called "the burnt district," the area that had been put to the torch by the Yankees. Everything, all the forests and hills, the fenced-in pastureland, the bushes and trees, was burned to a crisp. Not to mention the farmland and the barns and houses.

Some of the barns and houses still smoked. The district went on forever, it seemed. And it made one want to choke with the smell of it.

WHEN WE got to Seth's place, it was like coming upon heaven itself after days of traveling through hell. The world turned green again as we went down the only path in the burnt woods leading to it. Of course, the whole house being made of logs and concealed by trees, you could scarce see it. And you had to cross a creek to get there. But once in the holler, it was like another world.

Seth led the way, right down to the barn. And for an instant it was as if there were no war. All around me I could see crops in the fields, crops being brought in, wood being stacked for the winter. Seth dismounted and paused, his hands on his hips. "Maxine," he said, "gave orders for the winter wheat to be planted, and brought in the corn and potatoes, and has seen to it that the hogs got fattened. I saw some of it when I brought Martha home. But now it's harvesttime."

And then he saw a large figure in men's clothing coming out of the barn. "Maxine? It all looks beautiful."

"Sure does, Master Seth. Somebody had to see to it

or these lazy nigras you have here would spend all their time playing cards."

"How many people are left, Maxine?"

"Eight, not countin' me."

"So you're the overseer now?"

"Glad to give the job back to whichever fool wants it," she said.

"The Yankees been about?"

"They come once. Took two cows, so we got no milk, 'ceptin' what we gets from those two nanny goats of yours. Juliet, what trouble you got yourself into now?"

A nigra took the reins of our horses. Seth turned toward the house. "As long as the war is on, Maxine, this place belongs to Sue Mundy. She's a favorite with the Yankees. If they knew it was mine, they'd burn it. How's Martha?"

"She's tolerable, Master Seth. Walkin' 'round a bit more every day. Missin' you somethin' fierce. Juliet, you look like that bandage on your head went to war, too. Master Seth, Martha's on the couch in the parlor. She has a powerful yearnin' for some milk, real milk, sir. Know anybody who's got a cow to sell?"

"No. Look, I'll be overseer for the time I'm here. You care for the women."

"How long would that be, sir?"

"Two weeks, I'd say, but it'll give you a break. Juliet, why don't you go inside with Maxine and she'll fix you up. Maxine, this little piece of baggage here needs rest. Put her to bed."

"Seth!" I whined.

"No back talk, Juliet. I have enough troubles."

It was the roughest he'd talked to me since Sue Mundy had brought me back.

MARTHA WAS still hurting in her side and on remedies to help her heal. She was so glad to see us that I thought she was going to squeeze the lifeblood out of Seth, she hugged him so. Right in front of me, too. I have to say that Seth did his share of squeezing and kissing.

I didn't leave the room because Martha didn't want me to. I waited patiently. And when they were finished with this decorous hello, Martha pointed to a pile of clothing on a nearby chair. "I've been working on all that," she said. "And it's for you."

There were two dresses, two chemises, two night-gowns, and some underthings, all made out of the softest cotton. I thanked her and gave her my own hug, and she showed me a dress she was working on for herself. Then Seth sent me upstairs where Maxine was waiting to help me clean up and give me remedies for the cuts on my face.

He came up to see me when I was in bed in the room he had designated for me. He had something in his hand, held half behind his back. "I wanted to give you this," he said.

And he handed me the rag doll that had belonged to Charity McCorkle Kerr. The one Bill Anderson had taken from me. My eyes widened as I held my hands out for it. By now this doll had become more than a doll for me. It was the symbol of all I had been through, all I'd learned and suffered.

"But Bill took it from me," I said.

"I found it in his possessions when I sent him on his way. I took it back."

I hugged it close. "Thank you, Seth."

He came over and kissed my cheek. "Want you to stay in bed a couple of days," he said with another kind of roughness now, a roughness that meant fondness, a fondness he was almost ashamed to admit. "Hear me?"

"Yes, Master Seth, I hear you."

He tugged at my hair. "You get better," he said. "Those are orders from the captain. And oh, listen. I just told Martha what happened to you, how Bill kidnapped you. She's really upset over it. Don't bring the subject up unless she does." He touched his eye. "I had to admit that Bill and I had a fight. Just be careful what you say to her, all right?"

I said yes. I would be careful.

Chapter Twenty-five

I STAYED IN bed a full day to keep Seth happy. Then I got up and put on the robe that went with the gown Martha had made me. It lay at the foot of my bed. I felt so grateful for life, sitting on the edge of my bed, for the good people that surrounded me, for a friend like Sue Mundy, who somehow was always there to save my life, for a sister-in-law like Martha and a brother like Seth, both who looked out for me at every turn. I must be better to them, I decided. At least I must stop back-talking Seth.

Maxine wouldn't let me help in the kitchen, but I did set the table for supper so Martha could sit down.

"MR. ADDISON, down the road, has the only spread not touched by fire," Seth told us at supper a week after we'd arrived. "I hear he wants to barter for some things. I suggest we stay away from him."

"Why was he spared?" Martha asked.

"He's a Yankee sympathizer," Seth said.

"Does he have a family?" Martha pressed.

"Two boys, about eight and ten, and a little girl about three," Seth answered.

"What does he need for them that he wants to barter?" Martha seemed very interested.

Seth sipped his apple cider. "Two bear cubs," he said.

"Seth," Martha said sternly, "don't even tease like that."

Just after Seth and I came home, two baby bear cubs, hungry and motherless, had wandered into her kitchen garden where she was working. Martha delightedly took them in. But we had only goat's milk to give them and they did not fancy goat's milk. Maxine concocted a mixture of honey with the goat's milk, hoarhound tea, and catnip tea. The bear cubs scarcely drank of it and were losing weight. Martha worried the matter to the bone.

I fell in love with those bear cubs. Martha let me name them. So I called them Frisky and Tubby.

"To answer your question, dear," Seth told her, "he wants play-pretties for his three-year-old. Toys."

"Does he have a cow?" Martha asked.

Seth gave a short laugh. "I doubt he'd trade off livestock. Even if we did have play-pretties. Everything Juliet had was burned. Right, Juliet?"

I shook my head, yes, while inside my head I screamed no, no. There *are* things. *I have things. And Mr. Addison has a cow. Last I heard he had three cows!*

I said nothing, for it was impossible. Impossible for me, all of twelve, to negotiate with Mr. Addison. Why, I wasn't allowed to take Caboose and even ride out alone, according to Seth. That rule was carved in stone. But it did give birth to the idea that I'd best go and retrieve my treasures from where I'd left them that terrible morning Pa was killed.

That day, with the fire and Pa being buried, and us going to the Andersons and all, I left the box of precious things in the tree house. Likely they were safer there than anywhere else I've been since that day. And I fully intended to go and get them.

But how to get around Seth's brilliant order to not go out riding alone? I knew I couldn't fly directly against anything that was so clearly an order without incurring his wrath. So I decided to put the matter before him. Let him ponder it a bit and come up with a solution.

I did that evening, right when the house had quieted down after supper and I found him outside on the porch alone, smoking a cheroot.

"Seth."

"Umm."

"I need to know what you would do if you were me and you had this problem."

"The answer is no, Juliet. Don't even bother asking."

"But you don't even know what I'm going to ask."

"Now the answer is no with brown sugar on it."

"You said you would always be fair to me, Seth. You said that."

He sighed. "All right. Go ahead."

I told him. It did not go over too well.

"You mean you left Ma's good pearls in a box in your tree house since that day?" he asked incredulously.

"I never had the chance to go and get them."

He shook his head slowly. "Ma's good pearls. Sometimes I just don't know about you, Juliet. Is it your age or what?"

"Seth, don't scold. I have been through a few hardships since then, you know."

"All right. I'm sorry, baby. We'll ride over tonight and get them."

"Tonight?" I could scarce believe my good luck.

"Yes. We're both fugitives, Juliet. We have to creep around in the dark. Go and get ready. Put on something warm. It gets cold soon's the sun goes down."

I hugged him. "Oh, you're the best brother, Seth."

"Yeah, yeah," he said. "I know."

THE BOX was there, right where I left it. Seth helped me climb up the tree house ladder, and then back down. He put the box in his saddlebags and we set off the same way as we'd come, through the woods. Seth knew the paths where nobody else rode. We got back before ten that night, and I was allowed to take the box up to my room and enjoy my treasures before I went to sleep.

I examined my mother's pearls. I ran them through my fingers. Then I put them around the neck of the rag doll Seth had retrieved for me from Bill Anderson.

I got undressed and into bed just as Maxine came into the room with my nightly medicine. I took it without complaint, something that made her ask: "What you up to, Miss Juliet?"

"Nothing, Maxine. I was just going over my treasures."

She scowled. She did not believe me. She always knew when I was up to something, but she had no authority to make me tell her. And she seldom, if ever, went to Seth to tell on me. Trouble was, I had nothing she could tell.

"Don't ever ride out on your own." Those words stayed with me as I fell asleep.

THE NEXT morning was bright and blue and the leaves on the trees were near fully turned now. I went downstairs to breakfast, disappointed once again that I couldn't have real milk in my coffee.

Seth was gone already, outside to do the morning chores. I sat with Martha at the dining room table for a while, watching her write out the day's menu, working with what we had on the place. We had plenty of everything, except real milk.

Maxine had cautioned me to be good. Martha had had no success feeding the cubs this morning. Moreover, about ten minutes ago, she'd thrown up her own break-fast and begged Maxine not to tell Seth. Maxine was worried about her.

"All babies need milk," Martha said, "or they'll die. Of course some babies are fortunate enough to get it from their mothers. But if their mothers die or don't get it themselves before they are born, then you have real trouble. What was it you just said, dear?"

I had to stop and think of what it was. It wasn't im-portant. Words were forming in my mind, pushing their way around to make sentences. Decisions. Words that were important. Could a decision be made so quickly? Moreover, could I do it?

Why not? I had Ma's pearl necklace now. And I had Charity McCorkle Kerr's rag doll. I could barter for a milk cow.

"Is it all right if I go riding?" I asked Martha. "My horse needs the exercise and so do I."

"If you feel up to it," she said. "But remember what Seth said. Stay off the main road and don't go too far."

I got up from the table.

"You might want to change into boys' clothing," she suggested lightly.

I hesitated. "Why?"

She stopped writing and looked at me. "Juliet, do you recollect the day Seth came and got you at the hospital to take you to Quantrill's camp? Do you recollect how he made you put on boys' clothing first?"

I said yes, I remembered.

She sighed and looked me up and down. "Seth was taking you into a camp of men, tough and lonely men who hadn't seen a woman in a while. He knew the impression you make when you walk into a room full of men. He was protecting you. You are a very pretty young lady, Juliet. And Seth would be the first to tell you."

"I don't understand."

"He loves you, Juliet. An awful lot. And if he seems gruff sometimes, it's because he loves you so much and he doesn't know how to handle you. It"—she stopped to shake her head, then went on—"it *humbles* him, darling, to think he's been left in charge of you. And Seth is not a man to be easily humbled."

I looked down at my hands and nodded my head.

"So," she finished, "remember all this the next time you give him a difficult time of it. Now go and put on boys' clothes."

I got up, and then stopped. "Martha?"

"Yes, dear?"

"I'm not a little girl anymore. So you can tell me things."

"Like what, dear?"

"Martha, are you going to have a baby?"

Her face went red, then white. "What makes you think . . ."

"What you just said right now. About mothers not getting any milk before their babies are born. You weren't talking about the cubs. And Seth thinks part of the reason you're so smitten with those cubs is because you want a baby."

"Oh, he does, does he?"

"Yes. He says the doctor says you shouldn't, but what in purple hell do doctors know, anyway?"

"Juliet! Your language!"

"I'm sorry, but are you?"

"Yes. But Seth doesn't know. And he mustn't know. He'll worry."

"Maybe he won't go back to camp if he knows."

"That's just it. He's a captain. He's expected back. And he does want to go. I won't be the one to keep him.

I won't keep him here holding my hand all day. Please, don't tell him. Promise. Let this be our secret."

I leaned down and kissed her. I promised I wouldn't tell. I told her I'd soon be back, then I went to put on my boys' clothes and get my treasures, fully prepared to face Seth's anger when he found out what I'd done.

Chapter Twenty-six

I STAYED OFF the road, mainly in the woods, which were charred and burned. Didn't make much sense because I could be seen anyway, but at least I could tell Seth that I'd kept off the road when he found out.

I felt guilty already. Not because I was going against one of Seth's major rules, but because I was afeared that I was going to barter for a cow for the baby bears more than for Martha's betterment. Was I? This morning, after breakfast, I went to feed them with Martha's concoction in a bottle, but they pushed it aside and hid their faces in my arm and whimpered. *That's what pushed me to get the cow, as much as Martha's need.* And I was guilty about it.

Of course, in the long run, the cow's milk would improve Martha's health, nobody could deny that, could they?

Was that reason strong enough to stand up to what I was going to do today? And then there was the matter of my mama's good pearls. I knew Seth wouldn't take kindly to my bartering with them. They sat now in my pants pocket. The rag doll was in my saddlebag.

Good, there was the Addison farm up ahead, across the road, a gleaming white house with a porch, red barns, silo reaching up to the heavens, neat fences, horses and cattle, everything our spread used to be before the Yankees came. I pressed my heels into the horse's sides, crossed the road, and went through the open gate of the fence.

I heard the whizzing sound of the bullet before I realized what was happening. It went right past me.

"Halt out there! Identify yourself."

I couldn't see the owner of the voice, but I halted. "I'm Joe Mundy," I said, remembering the lie I was to tell if questioned in the outside world. The name Bradshaw was not to be mentioned hereabouts.

"What do you want, Joe Mundy?"

It seemed too important a request just to shout into the blue and gold surroundings. "I want to barter."

"All right. You can venture further in. I'll be down presently."

He walked from the front porch, two dogs with him, hunting dogs who sniffed me and my horse. In his arm he cradled a Sharpe's rifle, same as mine, the one I'd taken from off the rack on the wall in Seth's study. *There* was a hanging crime. But since I'd been taught to use one, I might as well carry one, right?

I prayed to God Seth wouldn't catch me with it.

Mr. Addison looked me up and down and in two seconds knew I was not a boy.

"You the little sister, hey?"

"I'm nobody's little sister. I'm a boy, and cousin to Sue Mundy."

"You people so muddled up in that house, so many comings and goings, you don't know who all is who all. Kin you take off the shirt for me?"

I clutched it fast in front.

"Thought so. You all is little sister to that Seth Bradshaw. Mean as a skunk in daylight when he wants to be. He home? Or is he hidin' in one of those trees yonder, ready to blast me away if I so much as look at you wrong?"

"I scarce know the man. Only heard his name. Heard he's with Quantrill."

"Why's your head bandaged like that? You get shot?"

Darn. I'd meant to remove the bandage. And he'd seen it beneath my borrowed brimmed hat. I gave no answer.

He squinted his eyes. "You one of those girls who was in that building what fell in Kansas City, ain't you? Kin to the Quantrill gang?"

I gave no answer.

"Just to keep things straight, though I'm for the Yankees, I think that was the worst sin of the war so far. Army got no business takin' things out on women an' girls. Hear me?"

"Yessir."

"Good. We got that straightened out now. What you want to barter for?"

"A cow."

"What you got to barter for the cow you want?"

"Does it give milk regular-like?"

He laughed, enjoying the joke. "You damned Southerners never give up, do you? All right. Come on up to the barn."

I followed him, leading my horse slowly. In the barn, he had three cows. All brown and white. All well fed and glossy. All needing to be milked. I had milked cows when I was a little girl, in better times. Seth had taught me.

I looked at Mr. Addison.

"Which one," he asked, "you willing to trade for?"

I just gazed at him, dumb-like.

"Oh, come on, you sweet little thing. I told your brother just last week that I was going to barter from here on in. What good does Confederate money do me out here? Maybe you ought to tell me what you got to trade, first."

I reached into my haversack and took out the rag doll. She looked beautiful, with her golden yarn hair all in place, her shoe-button eyes, and the big smile on her face. Her dress, newly made by me, was dark blue with red trim on it. Over it she wore a white apron.

He took it in his two rough hands, scrutinized it, and nodded approvingly. "What else?" he asked.

Now I dug into my pants pocket. Yes, they were there, wrapped in a man's handkerchief. I drew them out and handed them over. He carefully opened the clean and ironed handkerchief, and there was the pearl necklace that had been Mama's.

I heard him gasp, then whistle softly. "Where'd you get this?"

"It was," I stammered, "my mother's. She gave it to me when I turned twelve."

He held the pearls up, but there was no light to reflect upon them. "You sure you want to do this? I mean, they were your mother's!"

"Yes, sir. I mean, I love them and I love her, but we need the milk. We have no milk in the house. So what good are pearls if you have no milk?"

I heard a deep sigh, and then he pocketed the pearls and tucked the rag doll under his arm. "You're a good girl. What's your name? Juliet, isn't it? Hope that brother of yours appreciates you." He tied a halter rope with a bell on it around the cow's neck. "Here," he said, "she's yours."

"What's her name?"

"Daisy."

"I'm not Juliet Bradshaw, you know," I said.

"Sure, and the president's name isn't Lincoln. Listen, sweetie, I knew your parents. Only reason I'm trading with you and I never shot your brother. You look just like your mother. Now get before I change my mind."

I took the lead rope and mounted my horse and began the four-mile ride home, leading Daisy by one hand and holding my horse's reins with the other.

Daisy's bell jingled all the way home, slowly but with

certainty, announcing us. Best that way, I thought. 'Cause it's gonna be awful hard to explain this all to Seth.

And so it came to be that I brought home Daisy. For Martha, who couldn't quite admit that she needed real milk herself; for her two little bears, who were so greedy for it; and for all of us who missed it on our mush in the morning, and in our coffee and tea.

SETH WAS waiting by the open barn door. With Martha.

I could see by the look on Martha's face that he'd gotten out of her the fact that I'd gone out riding alone, that she did not know where, and that I was long overdue. I could see that his anger was there, in every pore of him, but controlled. His eyes were hard, his face set.

You don't ever want to be on the receiving end of a look like Seth was giving me then. The mouth curled down, the eyes were set like stone, and the whole face made you think that the sun had left us forever. Or rather, that it had never been.

I rode right up to them and stopped. He stepped forward and took us in, me, the horse, Daisy, and, yes, the Sharpe's rifle, all in one lightning swoop.

"Are you all right?" he asked.

"Yes," I said.

He held out his hand. I gave over the rifle. The cow mooed.

"Oh," Martha said, delighted. "Is this our cow now? Did you bring it for me? What's her name? Where did you get her?"

"Daisy," I said, ignoring Seth, who still stood there destroying the sun with his look. "I bartered with Mr. Addison. She's a real sweetheart, and she's all yours, Martha."

"Oh, you darling." Martha patted the cow's face and even gave her a kiss between the eyes. The bell jingled. "How can I ever thank you, Juliet?"

"Just having you for a sister is enough." I met Seth's eyes levelly.

"What did you have to barter?" she asked.

"Yes," Seth spoke for the first time then, "what did you barter?"

I spoke plain. I must sound unafraid. He wouldn't respect fear. "My rag doll," I said, "for the little girl."

Seth nodded his head, never taking his eyes from me. I was starting to get shaky. *I must control myself.* And my head was starting to hurt. *I must remain strong.*

"What else?" He took up the line of questioning.

"That's a prime animal. Would go for quite a sum on the open market." And I think he knew. I know he knew.

I started to speak, but my tongue got stuck and I had to start again. *Oh, God, don't let me get the mumblefuddles,* I prayed. "Mama's pearls," I murmured.

"What?" Seth asked. But he had heard.

"Mama's pearls." I said it plain.

He nodded, ever so slightly. *Oh, God,* I prayed, *let's get this over with. Whatever he's going to do, let him do it, and then I can run away if I want and never come back.*

He must have seen that I looked a little green around the gills, because he stepped forward, gestured that I should get off the horse, and then helped me down, steadying me. Oh yes, Seth, every inch the gentleman. Only now, standing before him, I felt small and vulnerable. Echo, one of Seth's farm nigras, came and led Caboose to the barn.

"Tell you what," Seth said quietly, "why don't you go on up to the house and wait for me in my office. I'll be along shortly. We have some talking to do."

"I'm all right, Seth."

"No, you're not." He spoke so low that only I could hear him. "You're the furthest from all right that you've been in a long time, and you and I, well, we have to figure out how to get you back on the trail now, don't we?"

I didn't like the tone, but I began walking toward the house.

"Seth," I heard Martha say as I walked away, "you're going to be good to her now, aren't you?"

I turned, briefly. He was going over the cow with his hands while Echo held the lead rope. "We have to settle some things, Martha, but yes, I'm going to be good. Am I ever anything else?"

"No. You're a good brother."

"You don't have to worry now. I've made you a promise that I'm not going to turn into Bloody Bill and I mean to keep it."

That hit me in the face like cold water, that Martha was fearful that Seth would go the way of her own brother and turn violent after the building collapsing in Kansas City and the raid on Lawrence, Kansas. I never had such fears. Should I? Bill Anderson had once been kind and loving like Seth, too. I went into the house and asked Maxine for a cup of tea. My mouth was dry and a whole pot of tea wouldn't moisten it again.

I stayed a long time that afternoon in Seth's office waiting for him to come in and "straighten things out" with me. I spent the time looking around. In as short a time as he'd been here, the place had his stamp on it already. Bookshelves on the walls. He must have moved the books before our house burned down. On the desk his writing things, ink and pens, ledger books open with records of the livestock and the produce grown on the place. A column of gains and losses.

Under expenditures I saw my name. "Payment to Martha for fabric for clothes for Juliet." And, "shoes for Juliet." And then something else that brought tears to my eyes. "Birthday present for Juliet."

My birthday was in October. He'd bought the present already!

It turned out that a rider came through the gate while I was waiting in Seth's office. It was a messenger from Quantrill with a note. I heard them coming into the house, so I quickly went to sit on the window seat with my tea.

Seth brought the man into his office. At first Jesse James, whom I'd already met, seemed like something the cat dragged in, all dusty and worn down. Seth had his horse fed and watered, even offered him a new mount.

Seth gave him some whiskey and was about to introduce us when he recollected we'd met before.

"You were in the building," Jesse James stated.

"Yes," I said.

"Glad you made it." Like all of Quantrill's men, he was polite to women. He talked a bit with Seth and then gave me a half bow and went to the kitchen to get the sandwich Maxine had made for him.

Seth came back into his office and sat down behind his desk. He pushed his chair back, his long legs stretched out in front. "He brought a note," he said. "I need to report back. Guess you'll be glad to see me go, won't you?"

I shook my head no.

There was silence for a moment. He ran his hand over his face. "I need a shave," he said. "Maybe I'll grow a beard. You think I'd look good in a beard?"

Where was he going with this? I decided I'd just follow. "No," I said.

He gave a short laugh. "Damned Lee has a beard. So does Grant. All the important ones have beards. Would you respect me more if I had one?"

Oh, so this was the way he was going to do it. Talk things out of me. All right then. "I respect you now, Seth."

"Do you? You scared the holy hell out of me this morning, you know that?"

I lowered my eyes. "I'm sorry, Seth, really I am."

He bit his lower lip and considered that for a minute. "Do you have something to tell me?"

I just stared at him.

"Because I think you do. And I think I know what it is. Not even you, who likes to go off on a toot once in a while and drive me to distraction, would chance going against my wishes like you did this morning without a good reason. If you have one, I'd like to know it before I punish you. Well?"

Tears came to my eyes. I drew in my breath and let it out again.

"Before the Yankees came," he said softly, "we had a fight and I practically disowned you and it got very nasty between us. Then you were taken prisoner, and for a while there I almost went nuts. I promised myself that, if you lived through it, I'd always hear you out before I went into a rage. So then, do you have something to tell me?"

"Yes, Seth, but if I tell, I'm breaking a promise to Martha."

"So it has to do with Martha, then."

I almost bit my tongue to stay silent.

"And you'd rather be punished than tell."

I nodded yes. "I promised," I said.

"Well, there's one thing in your credit. You'd make a darned good soldier for Quantrill. First, though, let me tell you what I think. I'm her husband, Juliet. I do know some things. And I know she's going to have a baby, though she thinks she's keeping a secret from me."

I felt the color rising to my face. Oh, I mustn't give myself away, but it was too late. I might not break any promises as a soldier, but I couldn't control the expression on my face. And he was watching me steadily.

"I'm not going to ask you to affirm or deny this. But I'd bet this farm that you got that cow so Martha could have milk to drink while she's carrying our child. No"—he put up a hand—"you don't have to say anything."

I looked at my hands in my lap.

"Look," he said finally, "it's better I know. I'm going back to camp tomorrow and if anything happens with Martha, you've got to notify me. All right?"

I sniffed and nodded yes, and still without looking at him I asked, "What are you going to do to me?"

"Well, I'm mad as hell about Ma's pearls. How could you give them away like that?"

"What good are pearls if you don't have milk?"

"Are you sassing me?"

"No."

"And I'm also mad as hell that you went off without a by-your-leave from me, when I told you not to."

"I told Martha I was going riding."

"You lied to Martha. You didn't tell her you were going out beyond the boundaries of this farm. I hate lying, Juliet. You wanted to barter; I could have gone with you or for you. So you have to be punished."

I watched him. He wasn't enjoying this at all. He was as miserable as I was.

"So every morning you will get up at six o'clock and go into the barn and milk that cow and bring the milk up to the house to Maxine. And every evening you'll do the same. *No excuses!* Got it?"

I nodded yes.

"I taught you to milk a cow, so don't say you don't know how."

He got up. So did I. For a minute we just stood there looking at each other. "If you were older, and a man, I'd offer you some whiskey," he said. "Anybody who has to put up with me deserves a drink of whiskey once in a while."

I gave him a small smile, but my eyes were welling with tears. I had to get out of here, and soon.

"You look after Martha while I'm gone."

I nodded.

"Well now," he said, "seems to me we handled all this like two civilized beings, didn't we? I mean Pa would have taken off his belt and had the back of your dress in tatters."

"I never loved Pa," I said. I'd never told him this before.

He nodded. More silence. Then without a word, he reached out an arm and I went to him. And he held me close for a full minute and no words were needed.

The next morning, in the mist and half-light, he left, like some character in a novel about knights and princes.

Chapter Twenty-seven

I ONCE ASKED my brother why he became a member of Quantrill's Raiders. He said, "We became bushwhackers to fight for Missouri without answering to a bunch of Virginians with brass buttons on their coats."

He said, "I know we do bad things. We raid, we steal, we shoot people, and usually Quantrill doesn't let us take prisoners. But it's war, Juliet. Look at what the Yankees do."

I wanted desperately to ask him how many men he had killed. Most especially in the raid on Lawrence, Kansas. But Martha told me not to. "That's not a thing a man talks about," she said. "If he ever wants to tell you, he will. But I doubt it. He hasn't told me. But I think it's a lot. And do you know what, Juliet? It was always in combat. Never once did he kill a man just to kill him. He did tell me that."

Not like her brother, she said.

Every so often she mentioned Bill with profound sadness.

And then, the last time he was home, Seth admitted to me and to Martha, "I'm getting tired of all the killing." And there was a look in his eyes that made me know he'd done more killings than even he wanted to remember.

"I think after next summer I'll quit the whole business," he told her, "and settle down." Next summer would be the summer of '64, a year after Gettysburg. The South already knew the scales were tipped in favor of the North. Seth told us that, too, before he left.

"The only action going on now," he said, "is guerrilla hit-and-run operations. And nobody knows if the South can hold out."

Eighteen sixty-four was an election year in the North. In the barn one day, I heard some nigras talking about it. We whites weren't the only ones waiting for things to happen.

———

But at home, things went on as usual. Every morning I got up at six, as Seth had directed, and milked Daisy. One thing Maxine taught me was how to make butter. I delighted in my finished product. When I brought the milk up to the house and she put it in jars, she showed me the rich layer of cream that formed on top. With it we could do many delightful things.

Martha made me a cake for my birthday and made icing out of the whipped cream. It was heavenly.

I wrote to Seth once a week, and when he could he answered. I thanked him for my birthday presents, a new woolen skirt and a copy of *Moll Flanders*. On the quiet, lazy farm the hogs were slaughtered the first cold day in November under the management of Maxine. The trees were all bare now and everything stood stark against an uncertain future.

The cold made it harder to get up in the morning. I took a lantern with me to the barn. And all along I'd been taking Seth's Sharpe's rifle. Nobody knew I could shoot it. It was my secret.

One day the first week of December, two riders came up the path from the main road.

One unmistakably wore blue, with shiny brass

buttons. The other was a woman. From the porch, I could see that the woman was none other than Sue Mundy, who'd been gone from us for a while.

"Does he look hostile?" Martha asked from inside the door.

"No. They're chatting. Like they know each other."

"Well, if it's Sue Mundy, I suppose they do," she said. "Tell you what, Juliet. Keep them busy talking out there while Maxine and I hide whatever Seth left around in here, will you?"

How much did she know about Sue not being a woman? Had Seth told her? Or did he keep her in the dark to protect her? He sometimes did that, I minded.

I stood on the porch, with an old jacket of Seth's wrapped around me, a civilian jacket I sometimes wore to the barn. I remembered that I was not supposed to be Seth's little sister, or know where he was, and the jacket helped me play the part. Seth Bradshaw's little sister would be wearing shiny button-up boots, several petticoats, and a fancy cloak with a velvet capelet around her shoulders. The Bradshaws were held in high esteem around here. They lacked for nothing. My pa had had money. Seth handled it now. I recollected him saying to

Martha on his last visit home that he was putting it in American dollars and depositing it in a bank in England.

The Yankee rode up, reined in his horse, and nodded up at me. "And who might this pretty lass be?" he asked Sue.

She had her answer at the ready. "That's one of my cousins, Maud, the one I told you about who fell out of the hayloft and near broke her head open. Maud, this is Captain Heffinger, come to visit for a while."

I said a polite hello. He doffed his Yankee hat. *My god,* I thought, *I'm a cousin to Sue Mundy! What have we gotten ourselves into?* But I followed Sue's lead.

She had Echo take their horses, then invited the Yankee into the house. He held the door open for me, and as I went past him I noticed his finery, his polished boots, his soft leather gloves, his spotless hat, his haughty demeanor, and I thought, *So the North wears brass buttons, too.*

Inside the kitchen Maxine was icing some ginger cookies. The Yank's face went haggard of a sudden. "My mother makes those," he said.

Maxine offered him some with a mug of milk. He actually set his hat down and sat himself down at the long wooden table and partook of the feast.

Martha came in. He looked her up and down. She was just starting to show her new motherhood by now, and he stood when she entered the room. "Ma'am. You a cousin, too?"

"Yes. I'm in charge when Sue isn't around. What can I help you with, Captain?"

"I'm looking for Seth Bradshaw. Somebody said they thought this was his place."

"I never met the man. My name is Martha Mundy. My husband was killed earlier this year at Gettysburg."

"Sorry for your loss, ma'am."

I did some quick counting in my head and thought, *Good for you, Martha, you've got the timing sort of right, anyway.*

"Maud here is my little sister."

"I had her down as the little sister of Seth Bradshaw, the one wounded in the building collapse," he said, looking at me. "That is a scar on her head, isn't it? Intelligence has it that she was taken to Fort Leavenworth to have her head stitched. And the brother offered five Yankee prisoners for her release."

"Captain, you doubt my word?" Sue Mundy could be a coquette when she wanted to.

"No, but something tells me these two women were

supposed to be on that wagon train out of Missouri." He stood up. "Thank you for the cookies. They're so good I might be back for more. Course in my line of work, you never know when. This is a fine place you've got here, Sue Mundy. Much obliged for the hospitality."

He moved toward the door.

"Hope to see you again soon," Sue said, smiling. "You dear man, do come back. And give my regards to the others under your command."

He went out the door. I let my breath out and only then did I realize that it was the first I'd really breathed since he'd stepped foot in the house.

IT WAS December and the days grew short and cold. Sue Mundy had taken off on a secret mission she could not speak of, and it was just me and Martha and Maxine in the house. Martha was tutoring me this year, as Seth wanted. A cough seized me and Martha became worried. She wanted me to stop getting up at six each morning to milk Daisy.

"I can easily get one of the farm nigras to do it," she said.

"I have to," I told her. "Seth said I have to, no matter what. And I don't want to go against him again." It was like a pact Seth and I had now. A pact we'd made without words. Like he was testing me to see if I had the mettle to carry through with his wishes. He'd treated me with decency, not allowing his anger to take over. And I had to show him I respected him and would honor my part of the relationship.

"Well," Martha said, not concealing her own anger, "just so you know, I'm writing to Seth today and telling him about your cough. And we'll see what he has to say."

I did not answer, but just picked up the freshly scoured milk pail and went out into the cold.

There was no other human in the barn. The horse stalls had all been cleaned, blankets had been put on the horses, and they'd been taken out to pasture to enjoy whatever thin sunshine the day would bring.

My position milking Daisy left me with my back to the barn door. The only sound there was came from the milk pinging into the pail. I thought about the day when I was about seven years old and Seth, maybe all of nineteen, held me in front of him and taught me how to milk a cow. How frightened I'd been, except for the nearness of Seth and the satisfaction of seeing the milk gush into the pail, just like this. I'd about finished now, when someone said:

"I see they're keeping you busy."

I jumped, coming out of my reverie. A man's voice. Familiar yet not. I half turned.

There he stood in the half-light the barn door let in. Bill Anderson. And a girl. It was his sister, Mary, who was sixteen, still bandaged up from the falling building incident.

"You're not supposed to be in these parts ever again," I told him. And I reached down for the Sharpe's rifle on the ground next to me. "My brother catches you, he'll kill you."

He gave a short, evil laugh. "Don't try to fool me, little girl. I know your brother is off with Quantrill, elst I wouldn't be here. Truth is, I'm here to see my sister Martha. Bid her good-bye. And see if she wants to come with us. I'm taking Mary here with me, back to Texas. Now you take me to Martha like a good little girl. Put that rifle down and I'll leave you be."

He knew I could shoot. He'd taught me. I saw Mary's eyes widen in fear.

"Put it down," Bill said.

But I did not move. Next thing I knew, I saw him go for his Navy Colt revolver at his hip and in a flash, fire it. Not at me, but at the milk pail on the floor. It made a terrible sound, echoing off the rafters, and there was a rustling of wings from some frightened barn swallows. In the next moment, milk was gushing onto the floor.

I cussed at him then, all my best cusswords, which I never dared say in front of Seth or Martha. And finished off with "You snake-loving polecat!"

He shook his head. "Such nasty language from a sweet little girl like you. Your brother ought to do something about your mouth. Now put the gun down or the next thing I shoot is the cow. I heard what you bartered for her, heard what you gave away. There ain't no secrets around here. Well?"

I set the gun back down on the floor, trembling with rage now.

"I know Mr. Addison, too, remember. And he's mindful of who you and Seth really are, and who my sister is, too. How long do you think it'll be before he tells his friends, the Yankees?"

"He's not a snake in the grass like you."

"Enough! Come along to the house and bring us to Martha. Now." He still had the Navy revolver pointed at me. I went.

Martha was just coming into the dining room to breakfast. She wore a blue silk robe Seth had given her, though he didn't say from where he had gotten it. Personally, though it is none of my affair, I think he got it from one of the houses in the Lawrence raid. That he'd stuffed it in his saddlebags along with some other loot, like a velvet dress of the right size for me. I've never worn the dress. I think I will, for Christmas.

"Hello, Martha."

He stood in the dining room doorway and she looked up, aghast. Her hand went to her throat and she wasn't sure whether to be happy or to throw a dish at him. But it was the sight of Mary that opened her heart. She got up, went to her sister, and they hugged and cried for a minute.

She didn't hug Bill.

He looked at her. "In case you're wondering, they buried Jenny at the Leavenworth graveyard with the other girls who didn't make it," he said. "Right next to Fanny."

"Someday I must go there," Martha told him. Then she looked at me, standing, white-faced and frightened. "Bill, you shouldn't be here. In this house. We know what you did to Juliet. It isn't right, and if Seth were to come now he'd kill you."

"I'm not stayin', sister dear. I came to say good-bye.

Me and Mary are goin' to Texas for a while. Till all this dies down. I came to ask if you want to come with us."

"Leave Seth?" You might as well have asked Martha if she wanted to have tea with President Lincoln. "Are you all crazy, Bill? Or only part?"

He laughed sheepishly. "When's the kid due?"

"Spring," she said.

Mary said nothing. She didn't seem to be present in full, actually, behind those eyes. I think she was in pain. Why was Bill dragging her around like this?

Thinking the same thing, Martha offered, "You can leave Mary if you want. Seth's a good man. He'd agree to it."

"You want to stay, Mary?" he asked her.

"I saw two bear cubs," she told him. "Outside. Romping."

He put his arm around her shoulder. "C'mon now, don't start. It's time for your medicine, anyway."

"They want to attack me. I'm afraid, Bill."

He fished a small bottle out of his pocket. "Here," he said to me, "take this into the kitchen and have Maxine give her a whole teaspoonful." It was an order. I looked at Martha. She nodded yes, so I took Mary by the arm and we went to the kitchen.

There Maxine fussed over her, commented on the head bandage, which was larger than mine had ever been, on the wrapped-up arm in a sling, and the way she limped.

"You should be in bed, sweetie," she told her.

"I remember you," Mary said, wondering how she could have.

"Course you do, darling." In two minutes Maxine knew she wasn't right in the head and made her a cup of tea. "You want some breakfast?" She had bacon frying in the pan in the hearth, coffee bubbling, and was ready to start cracking eggs over the skillet.

"No thank you," Mary said politely. "We have to go soon. Before either the bears or the Yankees get us."

Martha and Bill came into the kitchen. He wrapped Mary in a cloak and put a scarf around her head. Martha went about putting some bread and meat slices and cheese in a small sack for them.

He kissed Martha on the forehead and turned to go. I saw her shudder after that kiss. I saw her hug Mary. Then they went out.

"He shot a hole in the milk pail and it's all lost," I told Maxine and Martha.

"The devil doan always wear his green ears and tail" was Maxine's reply.

Martha just shook her head. "There's another reason you shouldn't be going out to that barn alone," she said. "Well, I expect an answer to my letter to Seth today. Come, let's have breakfast."

Just as she got those words out of her mouth came the sound of two gunshots, one hard after the other. I jumped. Martha put her hand over her heart and we ran to the dining room windows just as Bill and Mary rode by. Bill saw us and raised his hat in salute with one hand while putting his revolver back in the holster with the other.

"What was he shooting at?" Martha asked.

But I knew. Your heart knows such things. And I ran to the front hall and out of the house into the cold to peer into the patch of woods across the path, where the bears liked to play of a morning.

There they lay. Dead. Blood running down their beautiful winter coats.

"Noooo," I screamed. And then I went into a fit of coughing and crying. Martha came over to me, and she, who loved those bear cubs so much, held me close and told me that now they were running around in heaven. Where it wasn't cold and where they could find their mother.

I cried some more. "Dear God," she asked Maxine, who'd just come out the door, "what would Seth do?"

"I 'spect his bein' here would be enuf," Maxine answered her. "Leave her be, Martha, leave her cry it out. Come on in. Remember your own baby. She'll come in when she's ready. She's a big girl now. She'll come in when she's ready."

Somebody put a cloak over me, and I lay there on the cold ground.

Chapter Twenty-eight

"WHAT ARE you doing there on the cold ground, coughing your guts up?" the voice asked.

I must have dozed off. I recollect Martha begging me to come inside and me being sassy to her, then someone throwing a blanket over me. All I heard now was the far-flung call of birds going about their morning business. I raised my head. It was Sue Mundy, dressed as Sue Mundy. She was scowling down at me. I closed my eyes again.

"The bears are dead," I managed to say in a voice chilled with cold. "Bill Anderson was here and he shot them."

"When?"

"I don't know. Earlier this morning."

"Is that a reason to lie on the ground and sacrifice yourself to the gods for pneumonia?"

"I don't care about pneumonia. For all I know I've got it already." I coughed deeply. "Just go away and leave me be."

"You wouldn't talk that way if your brother were here."

"Well, he isn't, is he? He's out gallivanting someplace with stupid Quantrill and his men." I coughed again. My head hurt. I squinted my eyes in the brightness of the day. Who *was* that man a short distance from us, down the drive? He wasn't one of Quantrill's men. He wasn't dressed like it. "What'd you do?" I asked. "Bring home an outrider?"

"And I thought, when I kissed you way back when, it'd help you grow up. Well, it didn't, did it? Do you know what your trouble is, Juliet Bradshaw? Your brother never laid a hand on you, that's your trouble. He's too darned nice a guy. Go on, get in the house. I'll be along in a minute."

"I'm not going." I fell back on the ground and covered myself with the blanket.

Just then I felt a shadow fall over me, blocking the bright sun, darkening my world more than the blanket could. And in the next instant I was lifted off the ground, and a hand pulled the blanket from my face.

Oh, I wanted the blanket. *Give it back to me.*

The familiar face with a day's worth of beard grazed mine in a kiss. "Hello, Juliet."

"Hello, Seth."

"Stupid Quantrill, hey? Shall I tell him you said that? Or would you rather tell him yourself?"

I knew the smell of him, the strong soap he used mixed with whiskey and horse and tobacco. I didn't open my eyes right off because I wanted to throw up, I was so disgusted with myself.

"Come on, Juliet." He was walking with me to the porch. "Own up."

I hid my face in his shirtfront.

"I thought you liked Sue Mundy." In the house he paused in the foyer.

"I do." My answer was mumbled.

"You don't treat her that way. And the same goes for me."

"Oh, Seth, I'm sorry. It's just that things are so mumblefuddled around here."

"Mumblefuddled, hey?"

"Yes." I opened my eyes to look into his. He was not angry. He was amused. "And now the two bears are dead. Dead, Seth. That damned Bill Anderson shot them for no reason at all."

"Don't cuss. I don't like you cussing." Serious. Don't fool around with serious.

"All right," I said meekly. I am an expert at meekness when his mood calls for it. He set me down. Martha and Maxine almost leaped on him, and there were all sorts of greetings. In the next moment Martha and Seth went into a sunny corner of the dining room and kissed and hugged in front of the lace curtains.

When they finished she was flushed. I turned away and started coughing. Seth frowned. "That doesn't sound so good. Get my saddlebag, please, Maxine."

She fetched it and he fished around inside and drew out a small bottle. "Quantrill sent this for you. It'll knock your cough into next week. You gotta eat first, though."

"Everybody sit down," Maxine ordered. "And eat."

We sat at the table and everybody talked at once. I ate an egg, some toast, and tea. Then I kissed Martha and, without prompting, told her I was sorry for giving her a difficult time outside before.

"Oh, sweetheart," she said, "you know we all love you. Now go to sleep for a while. Seth said he's going to make little coffins for the bears."

Seth nodded and I kissed him. He said nothing. He made me take Quantrill's concoction right there at the table, a teaspoonful of cherry-tasting opiate syrup. Then I left the room with Maxine to go to bed.

"I know now how you manage her without raising a hand," I heard Sue Mundy say.

"How's that?" Seth asked.

"To the naked eye it seems as if you spoil her," Sue told him, "but when you really study on it, you've got her wrapped around your finger, Seth. But the cord isn't rope, it's silver."

"It's love," Martha said, "the strongest rope there is."

I looked back. Seth was holding his coffee cup and blushing.

When I awoke it was dark outside, night. From below I heard voices, ordinary family voices, and I smelled food. It must be suppertime. I quietly ventured downstairs.

Chapter Twenty-nine

THE NEXT morning we buried the bears. Seth had made two little coffins and dug a hole in the hard, unforgiving winter ground in a pretty little clearing where the bears had liked to play. Martha said she supposed it was all right if we said a prayer from the Bible over them. I couldn't believe my family was doing all this for me, for it was for me, I know, to heal my spirit.

My coughing had subsided. Whatever was in that potion from Quantrill had worked. "He gives it out to his men in the winter," Seth told us. "And by the way, Martha, I'd like to invite him for Christmas dinner."

Seth was to stay all through December and January. Quantrill and his men had made their winter camp at Mineral Creek in Texas, and he agreed to Seth coming home because his wife was expecting a child. And because a lot of his men were going home to Missouri for the winter.

Seth told us that many of Quantrill's Raiders were breaking away. "Too much dissipation and hooliganism," he said. "Too much time on their hands and whiskey to fill in the hours. There's been a breakdown in discipline. The old-timers, like myself, can't abide it."

He told us some went back to bushwhacking on their own. Some joined the regular Confederate army.

"And you?" I asked.

"Haven't answered that question myself yet," he told me.

After burying the bears, Seth attacked what he called the "traveler's room," the small room at the west end of the kitchen. He'd once explained to me that he and Pa had built it in a style after Patrick Henry's traveler's room, with brick floors covered with bear rugs, a buffet where food could be laid out, and commodious chairs next to a hearth.

"Pa's intention wasn't mine," Seth explained to me.

He was being helped by Echo. They were moving a double bed into the room. "His was for travelers. Mine is for emergencies."

"Are you going to sleep in here?" I asked.

"From here I can make a quick getaway if that Yankee comes 'round in the middle of the night," he explained. "My horse will be at the ready just outside the door."

"You're not sleeping in here without me," Martha declared. She had an armful of clothing. "Let's get the fire started, Echo. Warm the place up."

"The mattress isn't as good as the one on our bed," Seth reminded her.

"Then we'll take the one from our bed," she said simply. She smiled at him. He smiled back, and I saw how much they loved each other, how much it meant to them just to be together.

For Christmas, Seth set himself the task of making a cradle, thankful to Pa for forcing him to learn woodworking under the tutelage of Harvey, Pa's woodworker, who was still with us. We gathered holly in from the woods, and Seth cut a small tree. Martha and I decorated it with whatever we could find, including sugar cookies I made and popcorn.

I sewed him a new Quantrill Raider shirt for Christmas, though it was not to be a surprise. There was so much red embroidery on it that I couldn't stay alone in my room that long. Martha fashioned him a new pair of trousers. Seth gave her a new blouse and a skirt to wear over a hoop. He gave me a green and black plaid dress with the darlingest white collar. When we kissed him we didn't ask where he'd gone shopping. We knew he didn't want to be asked. And he'd say it was payment for Pa's house, burned to the ground. And he'd be right.

Quantrill never came for Christmas. A single outrider arrived a week ahead of time instead with a note that said he didn't dare leave Texas; his men were planning some mischief in the town of Sherman and he had to be there to keep a lid on the shenanigans. The rider also delivered two bottles of whiskey "rescued" from a Yankee supply-train wagon.

We had a sumptuous Christmas dinner.

We read a while later in the local paper about the shenanigans. Quantrill's men got drunk on Christmas Eve and rode through Sherman shooting off their guns, knocking off people's hats, making holes in church steeples, and blasting away at doors. They rode their horses into the town's only hotel and smashed into furniture, broke mirrors, and their horses' hooves broke the floors. The people of Sherman were paralyzed with fear. Quantrill had to send some of his other men to round the hooligans up and bring them back to camp. And the next day he sent them back to town to apologize and to pay for all the damages.

"Funny thing about Quantrill," Seth told us. "He's got his own moral center and it beats the hell out of that of most men."

Chapter Thirty

During the days now, Seth kept away from the house. Mostly he stayed around the barn or corral, working with the help. There was a new horse he was breaking in that he'd been given by one of Quantrill's guerrillas who came 'round to visit. Several of them did in the weeks after Christmas. They'd come with news, gossip, whiskey, and maybe a horse they wanted Seth to keep for them until "it was all over." Seth obliged.

When this happened, when one of his fellow guerillas came 'round, they stayed out in the camp Seth had constructed on the other side of the creek. There were a couple of tents, a rough stone hearth, a firing range, and plenty of food brought down from the house by me. Oft as not, I brought deer meat, ham, casseroles that Martha had made, potatoes he could bake on the hearth, even cake and ground coffee.

Always, I wanted to stay as they practiced their shooting skills or played a round of cards, but no, Seth wouldn't let me. He'd introduce me politely, then order me back to the house with some message for Martha. Always I'd hear the words *pretty* and *sweet* from the visitor about me as I went my way, and I'd know why Seth didn't want me lingering about.

Most nights when nobody was visiting, Seth would come up to the house and get in bed in the traveler's room with Martha. He'd stay for breakfast, take stock of what was going on, make sure I was doing my schoolwork, and go back to his work or his camp.

We had it arranged that if Heffinger or any other Yankee came along, I'd run out quickly and put a small quilt on the fence that surrounded the house. If Seth didn't see it, word would get to him and he'd skedaddle out of there.

Heffinger rode in on a Sunday night at the end of December, alone. He gave his horse over to Echo and knocked on the door, pretty as you please in his federal winter coat, with a gift wrapped in brown paper for Martha. Turned out it was yards of warm fabric to be made into whatever she chose for whomever she chose.

I escaped briefly to put the small blue and white quilt on the fence. Then realized it couldn't be seen in the early darkness. So I put on my warm woolen cape and my boots and picked up the Sharpe's rifle and made up some lie about going to the barn to see a sick mare. Then I picked up a lantern and, bowing my head against the cold, headed for the barn. As I passed through the kitchen, I picked up a piece of ham and bread and a half bottle of rum and shoved it in a basket.

I ran into Seth in the barn. "He's here. The Yankee captain. You better skedaddle. At least to your camp for the night."

Seth cursed. Oh, how I admired the smoothness of the words that had to do with hell being damned as well as purple, and naming God's son and calling him Almighty, words he'd have sent me to my room for saying.

Then he stopped and looked at me. Or rather the Sharpe's rifle. "Didn't I tell you not to carry that thing around with you?"

"No."

"Why do you? You can't shoot it."

I'd never told him I could. Only a fool would tell him now. "People don't know that. I feel that it protects me."

"Tell you what. You'll need protection if I see you dragging it around again."

Oh, he was good, shooting a bull's-eye with every word. I loved it when he went on like that because the words had no meaning. Yet I was expected to take them seriously.

I played the game. I handed the rifle over. It made him feel better.

"Better get back to the house. Thanks for the vittles. And tell Martha I'll be fine and to get rid of that son of Satan soon as she can."

"Yes, Seth." I kissed his cheek. He grunted and we parted.

On Monday morning Heffinger was still there.

It was on Monday that Sue Mundy hurt herself in the barn. She, or he, had gone down there to help Harvey, the woodworker, make a side table for the parlor. In the bright and dry morning air her scream echoed against the bare landscape and blue sky.

"Oh, hurry," Martha pleaded, as I grabbed my coat. "Oh, thank god Heffinger is still sleeping. Please hurry, Juliet."

Like a bat I was out of the house and running to the barn. There was Harvey holding some burlap around the forearm of Sue Mundy or Jerome Clark, his eyes big and frightened. "Doan know what happened," Harvey kept saying. "That saw just slipped. Doan know what happened."

"It's all right," I said, though I knew it wasn't. "Here, I'll get her up to the house and we'll take care of it. It's all right, Harvey, let go."

"Best fetch your brother."

"Ssh, remember, the Yankee is here!" I led Sue out of the barn and up to the house. There was blood all over my apron and her dress.

We walked right past Martha and into Sue's room, which was downstairs. *Remember, no one must know that Sue Mundy is a man. Not Martha, not Maxine. And especially not Captain Heffinger.*

Right off, Maxine wanted to take charge.

"No." I pushed past her and Martha. "I'm taking care of her. She saved my life. Twice. She's mine! Just get me some vinegar for her wound and some water and fabric to bind her up in."

"Juliet, you can't," Martha started to say. She followed me into Sue's bedroom.

"Why? I can do as well as anybody. Besides, ask her who she wants to help her. Go ahead, ask."

Martha asked.

"Juliet," Sue said. "My little friend, Juliet." She must keep her identity hidden, even at the cost of refusing expert help from Martha.

Martha shook her head in puzzlement and left the room. Then another figure appeared. Captain Heffinger.

"What's this? Somebody shoot her?"

"No," Sue managed. "I cut myself with the saw. Now leave me be, Captain. It's just a little cut. Maud here knows how to take care of it."

It made me daft, having to be called Maud in front of him.

"Well." He yawned. "Long as nobody's been shot, I suppose you three women can handle it. Maxine? Can I have some breakfast?"

"She might need stitches," Martha said to me.

"My ma taught me to stitch when I was five. Didn't

I make shirts for Seth? We'll be all right, Martha. Please let me do this!"

She agreed and left. I stripped off the top of Sue Mundy's dress.

"You don't go ripping off anything below the waist now, you precious little girl, you. And don't let anybody else in here."

"Do I look like I am?"

"And don't sass me. You're an impudent little thing. Don't know why that brother of yours don't put a stop to it."

A knock came on the door. "Here, cover yourself up," I told her.

Maxine came in with a basin of water, cloths, and liquor.

"No vinegar?" I asked. "And what'd you do with Heffinger?"

"Gave him enough ham and eggs and fish and coffee to feed his whole army. That's what that man needs. It'll keep him busy all morning. What this gal needs is rum to dull the senses. Liquor to wash the wound. You ever done this before?"

"No."

"I have."

Silence. "Whatever you got goin' here," Maxine told us, "you kin swear me to secrecy. Seth always did. I kept more secrets for that brother of yours."

Sue Mundy and I exchanged glances. "All right," Sue said, "but only you. Not Martha. Only get her in trouble. Seth knows, but he's not here."

Sue told her. Maxine made low noises in her throat. "Thought I done heard everything," she said. "Thought I done seen everything by half. Still doan know that I believe it."

Sue Mundy took the sheet that I had covered her with off her upper body to display the chest of a healthy midtwenties man. "Name's Jerome Clark, ma'am," he said to Maxine.

Maxine kept a straight face. "Ain't proper a young girl seein' such. But with a war on I suppose the lines are blurred."

"The Yankees can't know, Maxine," I told her, "or they'll kill him. They love him as a girl. And as a girl she's accepted as a Yankee spy. As a man they'll hang him. And all of us, too."

Maxine nodded. "Why doan you go in the kitchen and get yourself a nice cup of tea, while I stitch this up and put some laudanum on it."

Strangely, I welcomed the idea. But I was no sooner in the kitchen, getting a container of tea out of the pantry, when Heffinger came out of the dining room, patting his stomach and belching. "'Scuse me, that was some breakfast, Maxine. Did I hear something about the Yankees hanging somebody?"

He did not see me in the pantry. He went right into Sue Mundy's room, which was off the kitchen.

"What in purple hell?"

He stood stock-still, as I saw him from the back, staring at Sue Mundy, laid out on her bed, and Maxine wrapping up the arm. Sun flooded in the kitchen windows, like God's blessing, trying to filter out the wrongness of the scene but succeeding only in planting it firmly in my mind forever.

"Who in hell are you, masquerading as Sue Mundy?" he demanded. "What's this all about?" And he drew his revolver. "I left Sue Mundy in this room. Where is she and why in purple tarnation are you wearing a skirt?"

He strode over to the bed and pulled Clark off it by his good arm. "You better come along with me, son."

For an instant I panicked. Then sense flooded my whole being and I knew I couldn't let this happen. The Yankees will hang Clark. And Sue Mundy. And they'll find Seth and hang him, too, and maybe even me and Martha and Maxine, all my family.

I knew what I had to do, and I had to do it now. There was no question about it. That was Sue Mundy's revolver, wasn't it, hanging on a hook beside the hearth, where it always hung when she wasn't practicing. All right, it wasn't a Sharpe's rifle, but I knew enough now about handling and shooting a gun, didn't I? Sweet mother of God, I had to.

Thank you, Bill Anderson, I thought as I grasped the revolver and held it in my hands. It was lighter than I thought it would be, and I held it with both hands to keep it steady and aimed it toward Captain Heffinger, who hadn't even sighted me yet.

He was intent upon bringing Jerome Clark out of the bedroom. "Stop where you are," I ordered. "Let him go."

Heffinger looked up. The surprise on his face turned into laughter. "Put it down, little girl. And when I get time later, I'll spank you."

"I'm serious. I can shoot."

"Oh, so they taught you to shoot, did they? Who taught you? Seth Bradshaw? Then you *are* the little sister."

"And proud of it. Now release Mr. Clark."

Maxine looked as if she was going to wet her pantalets. She had both hands over her mouth, horrified. I felt horrified. I was looking right at the dark side of my moon now and I knew it. But I was not afraid. There are times you must look at it, stare it down, know what it consists of, know what you are capable of, and face it.

The Yankee laughed and raised his pistol at me and I aimed mine right at him, at his heart.

"You're gonna be sorry, little girl," he said.

At that moment someone shot a gun and the noise in the house was enough to make your ears fall off. I saw the Yank drop his pistol and clutch his chest with both hands, saw his eyes go wide, saw him crumple to the floor in front of Jerome Clark. In the kitchen all around me, crockery fell from the shelves and shattered, glasses broke. I heard the world split in half.

Seth. I turned, expecting to see him standing there behind me.

All I saw was Martha, eyes wide in horror. She held no gun. Nobody held a gun but me. My gun was smoking. I was the one who'd shot the Yank.

He lay crumpled on the floor, blood seeping from his body onto Maxine's clean wood. *Can you get bloodstains from wood?* I found myself wondering.

A door slammed. Now there was Seth, bounding into the kitchen, his own gun in hand. He took in the scene: Maxine and the half-naked Jerome Clark leaning over the dead Yank, Martha standing there trembling. He sat her down, asked if she was all right. He looked at me, saw the revolver in my hands.

"You shot the damned Yankee?" he asked.

"Yes." Now I was scared. I had done it. Would I be punished?

Gently he took the revolver from my hands and laid it on the table. He lifted my chin so I would look at him, and looked into my eyes. "Maxine," he said, "give my little sister some rum."

She moved, glad to be able to do something. "He was going to take away Jerome Clark," I told Seth. "The Yankees would come and hang you. Hang us all."

He nodded. "Drink the rum," he said, "and stop shaking."

I drank it and watched as he knelt on the floor by the Yankee. "We've got to get him out of here," he said quietly, "bury him, clean this place up."

"I'll help," said Jerome Clark.

"No, you take care of that arm. Maxine, go to the barn and get a detail of men to help."

She left. In a few minutes about six nigras were help-ing carry Captain Heffinger outside, and another three were cleaning up the mess. Soon Seth had them taking Heffinger's horse aside and getting rid of the saddle and all the tack that indicated it belonged to the United States.

"We'll rebrand him this afternoon," he said.

Chapter Thirty-one

THE HOUSE quieted down in the thin afternoon sun. Everyone went about their business. Martha made a pie. Maxine ironed clothes.

Sue Mundy (for she was in a nightdress again) called me into her bedroom.

"I would speak with you."

"Seth wants to, too."

"Seth can wait. He'll have you all his life."

I went into the bedroom as she ordered, closed the door, and brought a chair up to her bed. She was made up to be a woman in case the Yankees came 'round, and it never ceased to amaze me how she succeeded at this.

"Child, you saved my life. He was about to take me away. They wouldn't have bothered with a trial. They'd have hanged me as a traitor."

"But you're not a Yankee," I pushed.

"They think I'm a double agent." That was all. *They think*. She refused to explain any further and I did not ask.

"So I am beholden to you. You saved my life," she said again.

"You saved mine. Twice!" I said. "It was the least I could do."

"But you shot a Yankee! A little girl like you. And likely you saved all of them in this house, your brother included. Did you ever think of that?"

I nodded my head yes.

"Juliet, listen to me. I'm going to get better. If I take some laudanum, the arm doesn't bother me. I've got to get back to my work. I'll probably leave here within a day or so. I'll likely be back this spring, but the war will start to move forward fast now. The South talks victory, but reality is the word of the day. People are talking about how the South is to be welcomed back into the Union. All they talk about in the North is the abolition of slavery and the expansion to the west."

"How do you know?"

"I have contacts. Darling girl, one of these days it will be over. Your brother will be given a pardon and you'll get back to your lives. You may never see me again, so I wanted to tell you how much I think of you. How plucky I think you are. And I wanted to tell you always to remember these days and never to blame yourself for shooting that Yankee. It was something that had to be done to save many lives. And you did it. And someday you can tell your grandchildren about it So don't be sad. I know it hurts now, but it will go away. Just be proud. And oh, one more thing. Be good to that brother of yours. He's trying to do right by you. And he's a sweetheart. Remember, I said so."

She kissed me then, on the side of the face. And she gave me something. A ring she wore on her right hand. It had a red ruby stone in it. "To remember me by, child," she said. "Now go. Your brother is waiting."

SETH WAS waiting for me in his office, going over his account books. He looked up when I came in.

"I'm sorry I kept you waiting," I said, "but I had to say good-bye to Sue Mundy."

"You mean Lieutenant Flowers, don't you?"

"No." I stood in front of his desk, looking down at him. "I mean Sue Mundy. She says she's leaving in a day or so."

He understood. He nodded his head and didn't press the matter. He pushed his chair back, looked at me, and gestured that I should sit. I did. "I think it's good that you should put whatever meaning on all of this that you want if it helps you get through," he said.

"I'm not lying to myself, Seth. It's just that, to me, she'll always be Sue Mundy."

He nodded again. I know he was waiting for me to bring up the Yankee I'd killed. I leaned back in the chair. "Did you bury the Yankee?"

"Yes."

"I don't want to know where."

"You don't have to."

"That's what you can really call 'cleaning up after a mess I made,' isn't it?"

"You did what had to be done, Juliet. He'd have arrested your Sue Mundy, Martha, you, me, and god knows who else. They'd have come and fired the house. And it would have been back to step one all over again."

"So you're not angry at me?"

"Honey, how could I be? I'm not *happy* that you had

to shoot him, no. I'm far from happy that my little sister had to be the one to pick up a gun and end a life in order to save the rest of us. It just shows what an all-out messed-up world we're living in. At your age, all you should be worried about is clothes and boys and reading *Moll Flanders*."

He was right. How far had I come that I didn't recognize this truth? That I didn't rebel against it?

"The best part of your life," he said, "is being wasted in war. Your father being shot, your house being burned, you spending time in jail, then nearly being killed when it collapses, losing your friends who were killed, a man you trusted kidnapping you, having to give away your mother's pearls in order to get a cow that gives milk, Yankees occupying this house, having your pets shot, and now having to shoot somebody. Juliet, I'm sorry, honey, for what we grown-ups robbed from you. And if I could restore it to you, I would."

"It's not your fault, Seth."

"And now this business this morning. You having to make a split-second decision whether or not to shoot a man or let him prosecute and possibly kill us all. How are you holding up, Juliet? Last I saw you in the kitchen, you were shaking like a bird in a cat's paws."

I shrugged. "How am I supposed to *be*, Seth?"

He hesitated. He looked down at his account books. "It's like—," he said, and then he had to start again, "—it's like these books I keep. There're two columns, profit and loss. You enter the killing and then you enter what profit it did to people and then you enter the loss. Lots of times you don't think there's any profit. But that's only because it's too big a thing to fit in the profit column. Understand?"

I said yes.

"You live with it, sleep with it, eat with it, and walk with it every minute of your life for quite a while, Juliet. And then one day you find you aren't eating with it anymore and you think it's disappearing, but then it comes back just when you sit down to a good meal of steak and eggs."

"Seth, can I ask a question?"

"Sure."

"How many men have you killed?"

He hesitated only a minute. He meditated. "I've never told anybody this," he said softly. "I'm not like Bill Anderson who had to make notches in a ribbon to show everybody how many he killed. I've got the notches inside."

He bit his lower lip, then continued. "You tell nobody this. You hear?"

I said I heard.

"Thirty-seven."

I couldn't swallow for a minute. *Thirty-seven!*

"Except for five in Lawrence, Kansas, all were going to kill me. I'm not proud of Lawrence, Kansas."

We were silent for a while. "Honey," he said, "you have an advantage. You're a girl. You can cry."

That tore into me when he said that. I didn't know what to do, so I got up and went around the desk and put my arms around his shoulders and hugged him. I kissed the top of his head, as if I were the older.

"I'm going to rescind your punishment," he said. "You no longer have to milk the cow."

"I don't mind, Seth."

"But I do. Martha told me how Bill came into the barn that morning and you were alone there. I never thought about that danger. I was foolish. So beginning tomorrow you can sleep as late as you want. You've served your time."

He looked up at me. "If this business about the shooting gets too much for you, come to me. Anytime. And do me a favor, will you?"

"Yes."

"Don't grow up too fast. I need somebody to teach, somebody to bawl out once in a while, somebody to look at me just the way you're looking at me now and who doesn't see how scared I am most of the time. I have to say, the look is even better than the ones you were giving Sue Mundy."

"You were jealous."

"Course I was."

I thought, *If he's scared, then how can I hope not to be?*

But I knew. I'd be all right, scared or not, as long as I did as well as him.

What Happened Next

"Bloody Bill" Anderson: During the winter of 1863–1864, Bill Anderson took twenty of Quantrill's men and left Quantrill's command. He went to join Brigadier General Henry E. McCulloch at his headquarters at Bonham, Texas. Anderson usurped Quantrill's place as commander and continued with his raids and atrocities. In late October 1864, in Kansas, he and his men were burning houses, barns, crops, and murdering male citizens when he and a man named Rains charged through a militia line. Anderson sustained two bullets in his head and fell from his horse, dead.

His body was searched. Found was a "likeness" (photo) of himself and wife, Bush Smith, a lock of her hair, and letters she had sent him from Texas; orders from General Price; six hundred dollars in gold and greenbacks; six revolvers; a gold watch; a Confederate flag; and, lastly, a buckskin pouch containing a silk ribbon with fifty-three knots in it, one for each man he had killed in vengeance for his sisters.

Sue Mundy (Marcellus Jerome Clark): On March 3, 1865, Sue Mundy, Henry Magruder, and Sam Jones were holed up in a mud-chinked tobacco barn on the Cox place, forty miles southwest of Louisville, Kentucky. A retired federal infantry major by the name of Cyrus J. Wilson and fifty soldiers of Company B, Thirtieth Wisconsin Infantry, were dispatched and soon surrounded the barn. They threw rocks against the door. Sue Mundy blasted away and wounded four of them before they managed to arrest her and her two companions.

They were all taken by river steamer to Louisville, Kentucky, where Sue Mundy (Jerome Clark) stood trial, which was not a very fair court-martial, and she was hanged on March 15, 1865. An enormous crowd gathered as the gallows was built, and before the hanging Sue

Mundy said, "I am a regular Confederate soldier and have served in the Confederate army for four years. I hope in, and die for, the Confederate cause."

ON MAY 10, 1865, **William Clarke Quantrill,** with twenty-one men, was riding down a road that led to the Wakefield Farm five miles south of Taylorsville, Kentucky. It was raining, so they took refuge in the barn and carriage house. Quantrill and some of his men climbed into the hayloft to sleep. The others played cards.

Out back, over the hill, came twenty-year-old Captain Edwin Terrell of the Secret Service, who had orders from the military commander of Kentucky to kill or capture Quantrill.

A fight ensued. Quantrill was riding a borrowed horse, since his "Old Charley," who had seen him through the whole war, had pulled a hamstring. The horse he now had was not accustomed to the sound of battle or gunfire, and so became frightened and reared, and he could not control it. The animal was shot in the hip. A bullet struck Quantrill in the back of his left shoulder blade and lodged in his spine. He fell into the mud. He was paralyzed below the shoulders. His own men tried to save him but were killed. Men from the Secret Service rolled him in a blanket and carried him into the house. He lied, saying he was Captain Clarke of the Fourth Missouri Confederate Cavalry. Then he asked to be allowed to stay on the farm to die. Terrell said yes, then rode off to try to find Quantrill.

The next morning, having learned who his prisoner really was, Terrell returned with a Conestoga wagon. He threw straw and pillows in the back and put Quantrill on top of it and headed for Louisville.

There, doctors examined him and said his back was broken. He was put in the military prison's infirmary. As he lay dying, Quantrill was converted to Catholicism and given the last rites by a Catholic priest. He made arrangements that all his money be given to Kate King, his wife. He remained in a good mood to the end.

Legend has it that four women came to see him as he lay dying. One shed bitter tears as she left.

He died at 4:00 P.M. on June 6, 1865. He was twenty-seven years old.

AND—what I imagine happened to the characters that I made up.

Martha Anderson Bradshaw: After the war when Confederate soldiers were on the roads, some wounded, some lost, all trying to find their way home, she cared for them. She fed them, clothed them, and nursed them if necessary. Since President Abraham Lincoln had emancipated the slaves in January 1863, she and Seth had kept theirs on and paid them wages. All stayed, including Maxine, who still just about ran the place.

Martha had a second baby boy on June 9, 1865, two months after General Robert E. Lee surrendered to the North and the war ended. They named him William Clarke, after Quantrill. In the years that followed, she and Seth had four children, three boys and one girl, whom they named Sue Mundy Bradshaw. Juliet was her godmother. They raised their children successfully in the log cabin version of the house in the holler and remained a contented happy family and pillars of the community. Martha accompanied Seth to all the reunions of the Quantrill Raiders.

Seth Bradshaw: Lee surrendered on April 9, 1865. The war was over, although in the West many did not know it for weeks and weeks. On May 11, Seth led his men to a place a mile and a half outside Lexington, Missouri. At 1:00 P.M. he sent a messenger into town under a flag of truce to offer the surrender of his band. A colonel went to meet them. Seth had forty-eight men and they marched, on horseback, into town to the provost marshal's office, where they were ordered to dismount and turn over their arms. Then they took an oath of allegiance to the United States and all were permitted to go home—all but Seth. He was given the job of helping the military bring in the rest of the guerrillas. He took it to make up for the men he had killed in the war, going home occasionally to make sure his family was all right. By the end of May he had brought in two hundred to surrender. The last group he brought in surrendered on July 26, 1865. One guerrilla who never surrendered or took the oath was Jesse James.

Seth then went home to his family for good. Slavery had ended in Missouri by early 1865, by state enactments, and he had to hire some workers for the slaves who eventually left and check on the ones he had already hired. He had to see to his new baby and wife and his little sister, his crops, and the horses he had taken to raising.

At home for good now, he became, with Martha, a force in the community and, though public office was denied to all who had fought for the Confederacy, he became the "point man" for all those who had been driven out of Missouri by Order Number 11 and whose property was now in the infamous "burnt district." He helped them get their property back and start to rebuild. He also became unofficial historian of Quantrill's band, kept in touch with the ex-bushwhackers, and attended all the reunions. He lived until 1913.

Juliet Bradshaw: After the war, Juliet went back to school as her brother wished, in the local schoolhouse, then attended Miss Fishburn's Academy for Young Ladies, comparable to today's high school for girls, in the local area. Juliet felt that she had seen and learned more than Miss Fishburn could ever teach her, and that she'd poured enough tea for sick soldiers, on their way home, to teach Miss Fishburn a thing or two, but Seth made her go. She hated it.

She was thirteen when she fell in love with one soldier her sister-in-law Martha took in on his way home. He needed nursing and feeding and Juliet was hopelessly smitten with the young man, who was all of twenty. He was from Virginia. And if Seth hadn't been home, she would have eloped with him, but he was, so she didn't.

She had turned into a beautiful young teenager, with experience beyond her years. She loved her nieces and nephews, took piano lessons, and went with Seth and

Martha to all the Quantrill reunions, where she flirted with Jesse James. She even followed his career in crime, the way she used to follow the career of Sue Mundy.

But the Yankee she had killed still haunted her and was the real underlying reason for her wildness. (She once rode one of Seth's prized Thoroughbred horses without permission and almost killed herself.) And this was when the haunting of the Yankee came to the fore.

When she told Seth and Martha that she wanted to go to Pennsylvania to meet Heffinger's family and apologize to them, they were horrified and said no. "You're a Confederate," Seth said. "You're hated up there. Besides, you're only fourteen."

Juliet went anyway. She literally ran away with Heidi, the daughter of one of the hired help, a German girl from Gettysburg, Pennsylvania, who offered to go with her. They found the Heffinger home and were welcomed by a surprised and saddened family. Jeffrey Heffinger was the oldest son. His brother, Caleb, was home and took the girls on a tour of the still raw and ugly Gettysburg grounds.

He was twenty. Juliet fell for him. Before two days were up, an angry Seth arrived, ready to tear Juliet to pieces, but Caleb and his parents calmed him down, saying, "Her gesture was so beautiful, coming here to apologize for killing Jeffrey. It mended things so well. If all of us on both sides did this, it would help heal the nation."

When Juliet returned home, Seth kept her under lockup (she was grounded for a year), but she and Caleb started a written correspondence that, years later, led to marriage.

AUTHOR'S NOTE

Nowhere in young adult fiction have I ever come across the story about the Southern girls who were kin to Quantrill's Raiders in the Civil War being sent to a Yankee prison in Kansas City, Kansas, where the building collapsed and most of the girls were killed. The fact that most of them were teenagers gravitated me to the story. Why had nobody written about this for young adults?

I plunged right in and started my research. The result is this book, which deals not only with the prison collapse, but with William Clarke Quantrill's bushwhackers, as fascinating a group of beloved scoundrels as ever graced the pages of any novel. Of course they were Confederates, but that did not give them the right to burn, loot, and kill the way they did, unless you discover that they were only doing it in the way the Yankees burned, looted, and killed. It was war.

Along the way I invented as good a group of characters as I ever had with the Bradshaw family. And I developed a whole plotline with the introduction of Sue Mundy, the "girl" who disguised herself as a man and fought with Quantrill, the "girl" who was really a man to begin with and whom my twelve-year-old protagonist adored. Sue Mundy was a cult figure of her time. In today's world she'd be on the front page of all the supermarket tabloids.

As to whether Sue Mundy was really a double agent for the Yankees is speculation, invented by me to make her even more interesting. Remember, this is a novel *based* on the Grand Avenue prison collapse and the Quantrill bushwhackers. In that same mode the names of the Anderson girls (all of whom really lived) are as close as I can discern them to be. Every research book I read gave the girls different names and ages. Some had a Josephine in the group, some did not. I do not have a Josephine. So, if I am incorrect in my interpretation, please forgive me.

All the main characters in the book are real with the

exception of the Bradshaws; Maxine; the Yankee, Heffinger, whom Juliet shoots; and Mr. Addison, from whom she buys her cow. Jesse James started his outlaw career in Quantrill's Raiders, and after the war his brother Frank asked for a pardon but Jesse never did. He became, instead, a noted and infamous cult-figure outlaw of the times.

"Bloody Bill" Anderson really was nicknamed that, because after the Grand Avenue prison collapsed and he lost three of his sisters (Mary eventually died, too), he went crazy, literally. He really did keep a ribbon on his horse, with one notch in it for every man he killed. He kept, also, a collection of scalps. He killed and maimed unnecessarily. After his death, people came to stare at his body and cut off locks of his hair.

This was a violent, dramatic, romantic, and flowery time as far as people's actions and speech and emotions went. They held nothing back but gave vent freely to their feelings, as I have tried to have my characters do in this book.

BIBLIOGRAPHY

Berlin, Ira. *Many Thousands Gone*. Cambridge, MA: The Belknap Press of Harvard University Press, 1998.

Blake, James Carlos. *Wildwood Boys*. New York: William Morrow, 2000.

Faust, Patricia L., ed. *Historical Times Encyclopedia of the Civil War*. New York: Harper & Row, 1986.

Fox-Genovese, Elizabeth. *Within the Plantation Household*. Chapel Hill: The University of North Carolina Press, 1988.

Leslie, Edward E. *The Devil Knows How to Ride: The True Story of William Clarke Quantrill and His Confederate Raiders*. New York: Da Capo Press, 1998.

McDonald, Cornelia Peake. *A Woman's Civil War*. Madison, WI: The University of Wisconsin Press, 1992.

Ward, Geoffrey C. *The Civil War: An Illustrated History*. With Ric Burns and Ken Burns. New York: Alfred A. Knopf, 1990.